"Get ready!" Emma yelled as she ran closer to where Roger was supposed to be waiting for her.

She tried not to think about what would happen if he wasn't in position, for it was too horrible to contemplate.

Rounding a corner, she began to sprint, the finish line in her mind only twenty feet away.

Then she was there, running past Roger, who was standing with a pipe in his hands, the weapon raised above his head.

"Now! Do it now!" she screamed and dashed past him, the rats only seconds behind her, if that.

There had been no trial run on her plan; there couldn't have been. The instant Emma had touched her feet to the cement floor, the rats were after her.

Roger lowered the steel pipe like he was chopping wood, his target a pressure valve on a particularly large steam pipe about a foot off the floor.

The steel pipe struck the valve with a loud *clang*, the vibration riding up Roger's arm and into his head, causing his ears to ring.

Though he'd given it all he had, the valve didn't break, only bent downward.

The plan had failed—miserably.

"Uh-oh," was all he said as he looked up to see a horde of rats coming right for him.

NOW AVAILABLE AND COMING SOON
FROM
OPEN CASKET PRESS

HORROR CARNIVAL
BIGFOOT TALES
ZOMBIE BUFFET
CREATURE FEATURE
DECAY: A ZOMBIE STORY
DEAD CHRISTMAS: A ZOMBIE ANTHOLOGY
EARTH'S END: AN APOCALYPTIC ANTHOLOGY
HOLLOW POINT: A ZOMBIE NOVEL
WARRIORS OF THE APOCALYPSE: BOOK 1

RATS

RATS

RATS

ANTHONY GIANGREGORIO

- 1 -

Bobby Fisher was five today, and because of this, his mother let him go outside all by himself and play in the rain.

It was a steady rain, with no wind, and the gutters were flowing nicely in the small town of Wakefield, Mass.

It was a crisp autumn day but Bobby didn't mind. He liked the cold, and with his rain gear and rubber boots on, he loved to play in the rain.

As he walked down the cement path leading from his front door to the sidewalk, he held a small paper boat in his hand carefully.

The night before, he and his father had painted it with a water-proofer and he couldn't wait to try it out in the small rivers now flowing in the gutters.

Kneeling down, his hood on to protect his face from the rain, he gently placed the boat into the one foot wide river of gutter water.

Whoosh! The boat took off down the street, the slight incline making the gutter water become a tiny raging rapid. Though his mother told him he could go out if he stayed in front of the house, her warnings were already forgotten as he raced after the speeding paper boat.

The boat was holding up nicely, swaying from side to side but never faltering. It went over twigs too big to be moved by the rushing water and around the tires of parked cars. Billy ran after it, always a few feet behind, his prized ship just out of reach.

Boat and boy rounded the corner and continued onward and Billy saw that the boat was heading for the storm drain. The five inch opening was just large enough to allow the boat to go through, and he knew if he didn't reach it soon, he would lose it.

The drain was set up so it was basically a rectangular opening below the sidewalk, the darkness within like a small cave.

Billy ran faster, gaining on his boat, but just before he reached it by jumping into the gutter, ignoring the water rolling over his boots, the paper boat slid into the dark opening and was gone.

"Oh no!" Billy yelled as the rain pattered his head and shoulders.

As with most small boys, he cared nothing for getting wet, and he dropped down onto his knees before the storm drain. His knees and lower pants were soaked in an instant, the icy water chilling him, but he ignored it, his thoughts only of retrieving the boat, the one he'd worked so hard on with his father.

Getting down on his hands and knees, so he was on all fours, he reached his right hand into the hole, trying to feel if the boat had somehow gotten hung up on some refuse and was still attainable. When he felt nothing but wetness, he stretched his arm even more, sliding it back and forth along the drain's edge.

He was so desperate to save his boat that he pushed his arm all the way in so his shoulder was touching the edge of the opening. His hand was moving back and forth as he tried to find the boat but so far he was out of luck.

He was about to give up and pull his hand back when something suddenly grabbed hold of it and a sharp pain began on his wrist and shot up his arm till he cried out in agony.

It was a searing pain, like nothing he'd ever felt before. Well, there was one time, back when he was only a little kid—in his eyes that was a long time ago and he'd grown up a lot since then—when he was three. He remembered going to the stove to help his mother cook the pasta they were having for dinner. He'd tried to pick up the boiling pot of water but had spilled it. Luckily, only a cupful of scalding water had landed on his chest, the rest falling to the side and splashing across the kitchen floor. The pain of that moment had stayed with him for a long time.

The pain he now felt was three times as bad, maybe even four. He yelled out for help but there was no one around. The street was deserted, everyone inside on this wet and dreary day.

He felt the pain increase and he tried to pull his hand back but it was stuck on something. He didn't know what it was but it was warm…and wet. Not the kind of wet from the rain. This was more…*moist* was the word that came to mind.

He called out for help again but once more no one came to his aid. Tears were rolling down his cheeks, lost amidst the drain water splashing his face.

He managed to pull his arm out just a little, and thought that maybe he was going to get free, but then he was yanked back so hard his head hit the curb. Luckily for Billy, his forehead struck with such force that he was immediately knocked unconscious, and thus, was saved the agony as to what was about to come next.

If someone had been watching from afar, they would have seen a small boy with his arm sticking into the storm drain, but if they had continued to watch, they would have seen the boy suddenly jerk forward, then go limp.

As the body slumped to the ground, whatever was tugging on it continued its actions. With what had to be superhuman strength, the body was pulled into the storm drain an inch at a time. The head wouldn't fit and was bent backward at an odd angle until it was horizontal with the boy's shoulder blades. The body went slack and then another mighty jerk pulled it deeper into the hole. The sound of bones breaking filled the air, overriding the steady patter of the rain. The left arm was bent backwards until it snapped out of its socket.

That was when Billy woke up, the pain enough to snap him out of his unconsciousness.

He resembled a human pretzel now, his arm over his head, his head almost upside down, his legs limp behind him. He was halfway into the drain, and his blood was seeping out of his mangled body to mix with the rainwater. His terrified and anguished screams were truly epic, reaching shrieking proportions as he was tugged and yanked into the storm drain.

It was only when his spine snapped that his screams ceased and the now still body was pulled one last time into the drain, to slip into the hole as if it was greased; the blood doing just that.

In seconds, the blood from the boy's crushed body was washed away to be lost in the storm drain.

A minute after the body was sucked into the opening, the door to a house across the street was thrown open and a heavy-set old woman rushed outside.

She was wearing a housecoat but had on rubber boots, a yellow umbrella keeping her relatively dry. Her eyes were wide as she searched the rainy street, searching for the origin of the screams she'd heard only seconds ago. She walked to the sidewalk and stood over the storm drain, the tips of her boots almost touching where Billy's head had struck the curb, the blood now scrubbed clean by the rain.

There was nothing to be seen, only a quiet neighborhood, as it always was.

Deciding she must have been imagining it, she turned and quickly waddled back inside, where it was warm and dry.

If she had stayed on the sidewalk for just a few more seconds, it was possible she might have heard the sound of crunching and breaking bones, of the mastication of meat as it was torn from small bones, as what waited beneath the small town fed on the five-year-old boy.

- 2 -

The next morning, as half the town was searching for Bobby Fisher, assuming it was a child abduction, Zachery Jorgensen was walking to school. His mother and step-father hadn't watched the news the previous night or this morning, or else they never would have let their nine-year-old son walk to school alone. But Zach was mature for his age and his parents both worked, so it was easier on them if he walked to school by himself.

Besides, he had his cell phone in case he ran into trouble.

Zach was looking forward to school this morning. In his back-pack, he had his favorite show-and-tell item with him. It was a petrified rock he'd found when he was on vacation with his parents in the White Mountains of New Hampshire two years ago. He didn't know why he cherished the rock so much; perhaps it reminded him of a happier time, when it was just him, his mother and his real father…well, before the divorce and his dad had moved to New York.

Not that his step-father was so bad, but no matter what, Paul wasn't his 'real' father. He missed his real dad badly but as he was only nine, he was helpless to do anything about it.

At least he had the summers to spend with his father but that was over seven months away. Christmas would be coming in a few months but it was always awkward with Paul around, too.

It just wasn't the same as it was years ago when his parents were still married.

Zach turned and cut down a long alley, tall buildings on each side. The fronts of the buildings were anything from a hair salon to a small diner.

As he walked, he could smell bacon cooking and other odors of the businesses they were attached to.

It was as he walked by a sewer grating, the ground still wet from the previous day's soaking of torrential rain, that he heard a squeaking sound.

His curiosity peaked, he bent down and tried to hear the noise better. It was faint and it made him think of a kitten. As he waited to hear it again, an airplane flew overhead and a police car sped past the end of the alley, only its lights flashing.

All the noise caused him to lose his concentration, and after seconds ticked by and still no sound, he decided it wasn't worth the trouble and prepared to continue on his way to school. He had taken no more than two steps when the sound came from the grating again.

He stopped walking and his head swiveled like an owl's, and he stared at the grating again.

Was it his imagination or could he see two glowing eyes within the darkness of the sewer opening?

Being a kid, there was no fear in Zach, only more curiosity. Going down on his knees, he leaned closer to the opening so he could see better.

"Here, kitty, kitty," he said, his voice high and cute. If Zach had one thing going for him, it was that he was cute. All his teachers loved him and he had many friends as well.

His face was only inches from the grating, the smell of wet, decaying leaves and other moist items that had found their way underground filling his sinuses. He didn't mind, he was too focused on the kitten in the sewer.

He already had visions of bringing it to school and showing it off for show-and-tell. Then he would bring it home and beg his mother to let him keep it. Of course she would balk at first, but after he pleaded and he'd shed a few fake tears, he had no doubt she would come around.

Why, if he felt the need, he would even drop the whole 'you got divorced because of me' if it came right down to it. He may have been nine, but he wasn't stupid.

Some of the other kids he knew in school were from divorced parents, and they'd told him the tricks of the trade, how to get what he wanted by simply using his mother and father's guilt over breaking up.

Another police car zoomed past the alley, this one with its siren on.

Zach peered into the darkness, searching for the kitten. His eyes were wide as he tried to take in all the light he could and break through the wall of blackness, when something darted out of the darkness and sank its teeth into his nose.

He screamed and tried to pull back, but whatever had him was heavy, so heavy he couldn't move. He managed to move back a few inches, and when he did, the morning light cast his attacker in full view.

Zach's eyes focused on the face of the giant rat no more than an inch from his own. The rat still had his nose in its teeth and Zach began to taste blood as it dribbled down his throat.

Grabbing the rat by its side, he cried and tried to pull it off him. But the rodent would have none of it and it sank its teeth even deeper, cartilage crunching under its powerful jaws.

Zach began to panic and his fists started to punch the rat. He peed himself in his terror and pain but still the rodent wouldn't let go. Then, another came out of the sewer grate and sank its teeth into his right cheek.

Flesh tore and ripped as the rat began to burrow into Zach's mouth, causing him to gurgle his next scream.

Zach's knees went out from under him and he hit the ground hard as the two rats began to drag him into the sewer opening. Half his face was missing thanks to the rat feeding on his cheek and his nose was quickly torn off, the rat sucking it down and then going in for more.

This time the rodent sank its incisors into his lower lip, cutting it in half and peeling it off like the piece of skin off a cooked chicken.

Zach was crying heavily, his eyes wide with pain as he watched the rats feed on his face from inches away. His legs were kicking up and down as he was slowly dragged into the sewer.

When half of Zach's body was in the opening, more rats came out of the darkness and began to feed. Though they tried to pull the boy into the hole, he wouldn't fit, Zach's backpack stopping his forward momentum.

Working as a team, the rats began to chew at the boy's waist, burrowing into the meat and organs within. Zach managed one more sputtering cry before going still, blood loss and shock finally too much for his consciousness, which was mercifully lost.

The rats fed until they had sliced the boy in half, and with one mighty yank, they pulled the upper half of the body into the sewer. Leaving the lower half jammed in the grating.

The body was quickly pulled into the darkness where the sounds of mastication continued.

Ten minutes after Zach had been bifurcated, his lower half laying there as it cooled in the morning sun, one of the back doors to a local business opened and a man wearing an apron exited, a black trash bag in each hand.

Walking across the alley, he opened the dumpster and dropped the bag into the container, then pulled out a pack of cigarettes to get in a quick smoke before returning inside. He needed to drain the deep fat fryer, clean the grill and wash the vents, so he wanted to get in a quick smoke before diving into his chores.

As he lit up, his eyes scanned the alley and he spotted the oddest thing he'd ever seen. About twenty feet away, a boy appeared to be stuck in a sewer grating.

"Hey, kid, you need help?" he called, taking a drag on his cigarette.

Maybe the kid had dropped his lunch money and it had rolled into the sewer, he thought. When the boy didn't respond, he crossed the alley and walked up to the kid and that was when he saw what sure as hell looked like blood beneath the body.

"Hey, kid, you all right?" he asked again as he reached down and grabbed the boy by his backpack. When he yanked it back, he was surprised at how light the body was, but quickly found out why when he saw there was no top to the kid, only a jagged wound where organs spilled forth, intestines splashing onto the ground.

He promptly dropped the body and threw up, and continued to dry heave for more than three minutes before he had it together enough to crawl away a few feet and lean against the bumper of a car.

When he thought he could talk without wanting to vomit again, he pulled out his cell phone and called the police, knowing when they arrived, they were never going to believe this.

Hell, he was standing a few feet from the body and *he* still didn't believe it.

- 3-

Wild dogs.

That was the headline in the newspaper the next day. A rare occurrence but a possible one, at least to explain the brutal attack on Zach.

The article said that wild dogs had attacked a child named Zachery Jorgensen, and the police were looking into the possibility that Bobby Fisher had been attacked as well, only his body hadn't been found.

Volunteers were roaming the small town, searching for any signs of the feral animals but so far nothing had been discovered.

Parents were warned to watch their children, especially the smaller ones, as wild dogs were more apt to attack children than adults, as children would be considered weaker and more vulnerable.

Susan Mills was running late and had missed the bus, so she'd decided to walk home instead, not wanting to wait another hour for the next one. She had gone into the city to visit her sister and was now looking forward to a warm bath and a good meal.

Of course, all this would be after she put her child to bed. Susan was pushing a baby stroller, her daughter Bekah sleeping soundly, smothered in blankets. It was a cool night and Susan didn't want Bekah to catch a cold.

Bekah was all of two years old, with light red hair and a smile that lit up a room. Susan had dark hair and she joked that some rust must have gotten into her egg when Bekah was conceived.

When asked about the father, Susan would quickly change the subject. Jared was an asshole, and when he'd been told he was going to be a daddy, he'd quickly taken off for Florida, leaving her to raise the child on her own.

Not that she minded. He hadn't been such a great catch to begin with.

Besides, she was an independent soul, and was more than capable of raising Bekah by herself. She had come from a military family and had learned to shoot at an early age, her father and her brother taking her on hunting trips almost every weekend.

And that was why Susan was walking through the park at night, even though she was well aware of the warnings of roving wild dog packs.

In her purse, she carried a small pistol, one she had taken to the firing range on multiple occasions. If some wild dogs tried to attack her or hurt Bekah, she wouldn't hesitate to shoot them dead.

It was as she was walking over a small foot bridge that she suddenly stopped and looked around her. She could have sworn she heard scraping, such as claws on cement.

Slowly reaching into her purse, she pulled out her gun, her ears straining to hear any more sounds. Her eyes darted back and forth, trying to pick up a visual if there was someone, or something, in the park stalking her.

She was a few feet from the closest street lamp and the surrounding park was wreathed in darkness.

The hair on the back of her neck began to rise and she swallowed a knot in her throat. Suddenly, she didn't feel so confident, and in fact, she felt very vulnerable.

Bekah made a few noises in her sleep, the whimpers seeming loud in the darkness.

Susan decided the safety of Bekah was more important than acting brave and she began to run, pushing the stroller in front of her, its plastic wheels loud as they rolled over the pavement.

It was when she reached the end of the foot bridge that something darted out from the shadows and nipped at her right ankle. It was there one moment, and an instant later was gone, lost in the darkness.

Susan cried out and stumbled, falling to the ground. The stroller rolled for another four feet before one of the front wheels hit a rock and it fell onto its side. Buckled into the stroller, Bekah began to howl in fear as her world suddenly turned sideways.

Susan began crawling to Bekah, wanting to comfort her child, but before she could move a foot, more shadows burst out of the darkness and swarmed over her.

They were as big as small dogs and at first that's what she thought they were, but when a sliver of moonlight slid through the canopy of trees, she saw they weren't dogs at all, but rats…giant rats.

The smallest one was at least two feet long, not including the tail, their heads the size of large housecats. On the left ear of each one, something shiny reflected the wan light.

That was all she had time to see before they covered her from head to toe. There were at least six, perhaps more, as there was no way she could count, but she felt each bite and scratch as they attacked her.

Still holding her gun, she fired three rounds, hitting two in the side and missing with the last bullet. Two rats squealed in pain but continued to attack her. Then sharp teeth sank into her wrist and the gun fell from numb fingers.

Punching and kicking, she did her best to fight off the giant rodents, knowing if she was going to save her baby, first she needed to save herself.

But there were simply too many.

She pushed one away, and another darted in and sank its teeth into her throat, then yanked back its head. Blood spurted upward as her carotid was severed and she began to choke and gasp, the warm blood splashing into her face as it squirted out of her with each beat of her heart.

Bekah's high-pitched scream came to her ears and Susan rolled over to see three rats clawing at the baby stroller. She tried to call out, hoping to scare them away, but all that came out were bloody bubbles of red froth.

Her eyes wide in terror for her child, Susan could only lay there and watch her baby pulled from the stroller and dragged off into the darkness.

With a surge of renewed energy in her last seconds on Earth, she tried to stand, but the weight of the rodents on top of her were too much and she barely managed to lift her body an inch off the ground before falling back to the pavement.

As her eyes began to close in death, the last thing she heard were Bekah's cries ceasing and then the sound of small bones cracking.

Tears rolled down Susan's cheeks as she faded into oblivion.

The rats continued to feed on Susan, but as soon as they began, they stopped. The meat didn't taste like the two others humans they'd attacked and eaten the previous day, the smaller ones.

The meat of this one tasted tough and not as sweet. One rat with a larger silver tag on its ear than the others looked up and chattered to the group, the rest understanding immediately.

The large humans tasted foul, it was the small ones they needed to keep killing. They were young and tender and the meat melted in their mouths.

As one group they jumped off the body and ran into the shadows, in the direction the baby had been dragged. That small human had been very young and all the rats knew the meat would be the sweetest of all.

Unknown to the rats, they had become as discerning as humans when it came to what they ate.

The town's young had become to the rodents what veal was to humans...and they were all very hungry.

- 4 -

Two hours after Susan Mills was killed and the police were just arriving on the scene to try and piece together what had happened, eleven year old Domenic Salvatore was on the other side of town, making his way home as well.

He had been hanging at a friend's house and was supposed to have left before dark but had got caught up in the video game he and his friend Chad were playing and had lost track of time.

So now he was going home in the dark, something his parents wouldn't have been pleased about. With the recent attacks, they would have demanded he get a ride either from them or even a cab. But then they would have known he hadn't gone home when he was supposed to.

Luckily, they were both working late and didn't know he wasn't home yet. He didn't notice the small flyer on the telephone pole as he passed it. On the flyer, Bobby Fisher's face was smiling, the words below asking if anyone had seen him and to call the phone number listed if he was spotted.

His cell phone rang and he pulled it out of his coat pocket. Seeing the ID, he opened it and said, "Hi, Mom, what do you need?"

"Nothing, dear, just checking up on you."

"I'm fine," he said, controlling his breathing as he walked. He didn't want her to hear him or she would know he wasn't home.

"Is your father home yet?" she asked.

Domenic bit his lip. If he was and he said no, he would be caught in a lie, but then if his father had gotten home before him, then it was all over anyway; he'd be in trouble, so he decided to just go with, "No, he isn't. It's just me."

"Did you eat dinner yet?" she asked.

"No, in a few minutes." Then he asked what he really needed to know. "When will you be home?"

There was a pause as his mother no doubt checked her watch and did some figuring in her head. "About an hour or so. Make sure all your chores are done before you sit down to watch TV for the night. No video games till it's all done."

"Yes, Mom," he said, rolling his eyes. The same thing every day, the same speech, too. He'd heard it so many times he could repeat it verbatim.

Another voice could be heard in the background and his mother's voice grew faint as she talked to someone else. A second later she said, "Okay, Dom, I have to go. I'll see you soon. Make sure the doors are locked and don't go outside for anything. you know about the dog attacks."

"Yeah, Mom, I hear ya," he said.

"I love you," she said.

"Uh-huh," was his bored reply. He closed the cell phone, ending the call, and shoved it back into his pocket.

Moms, they never let up, not even for a second.

It was a big city and the odds that those so-called wild dogs would find him as he made his way home was astronomical. Besides, he was a kid, nothing bad could happen to him. Sure, the other kids had had bad stuff happen to *them*, but that was different. He was Domenic Salvatore, he was *immortal*.

15

He reached a corner and looked around, knowing he had a choice to make. He could go straight and then take a right, or he could take a right at this moment and cut through the alley that separated North and West Street.

If it was still light out, the alley would have been a no-brainer but now, with darkness having fallen and his mother's words about not being out so late, he was a little hesitant.

But he knew his father could be only minutes away from home and he needed to beat his dad there or else he'd be grounded… again.

So there was really no choice when it came right down to it.

Turning, he began walking down the alley, his eyes snapping back and forth as he tried to peer into the shadows on all sides.

Trash barrels lined each side, looking like tiny soldiers in the darkness. Domenic wanted to start running, but a primordial fear made him simply walk slowly.

Deep down he knew if he ran, then something could easily jump out of a corner or from an alcove and attack him, and he'd never see it coming. No, better to walk slowly, take each step carefully, his ears straining to hear a noise or sound that would signal danger the entire time.

From somewhere far off he could hear voices. They were male, and if he had to guess it sounded like they were arguing. Then the voices stopped suddenly. He knew there was a bar a street over.

The redolence of rotting food came to him and he walked more to the left, not wanting to get too close to the dumpster on his right. Nearby, a sewer grate yawned like a rectangular, toothless mouth and a manhole cover steamed softly in the cool air before him.

Feeling a chill run down his back, he picked up his pace a little more, not running and not jogging, but more of a fast walk.

It was as he passed by the dumpster that something scurried out into the center of the alley. It was low to the ground and at first he thought it was a large cat, but as he stepped a few feet closer, he saw the muzzle was all wrong, and the tail was thin, like rope, not furry like a cat's.

The words, *wild dogs*, came into his mind, but as he stared at the small shape, he knew it wasn't a dog.

Then another one scurried out and joined the first, then another and another until there were at least six or seven of the things. It was hard to count them in the darkness and they blended in easily.

Not wanting to deal with the animals, he turned around, figuring he would dash out of the alley the way he'd come and then get help, but as he spun about, he saw four more shapes blocking his retreat. He was trapped.

His heart began to beat faster as adrenalin flooded his system. He reached into his pocket slowly to pull out his cell phone, but as he did, his fingers wouldn't cooperate and the phone slipped through his grasp to clatter on the ground. He was about to try and pick it up, already crouched down and reaching for it, when one of the shapes zipped by him and snatched the phone in its mouth.

It happened so fast Domenic never knew it happened till the creature was gone and he'd yanked his hand back in fear.

When the shape had darted past with the cell phone in its mouth, Domenic had felt the thing's fur. It was only for the briefest of seconds but it was enough to know the hair had been coarse and short, and where it had touched him his skin felt oily.

It was still too dark in the alley to see the shapes clearly, but then a car did a U-turn at the end of the alley and for just a second or two, the alley was awash with white light. Then the light was gone as the car continued on its way.

Domenic had used that brief illumination wisely, and in that flash of light, he'd seen the bodies of more than half a dozen rats, all three times the size of normal ones.

There had been something reflective, like metal, on each of their ears as well, but he only took this in unconsciously, for he was frozen in shock at seeing the large rodents before him.

Swallowing the large knot in his throat, he could feel tears welling up in his eyes. He fought them back down; something inside him telling him that he needed to keep it together, or he would end up like Zachery Jorgensen, who the entire town was talking about.

One of the rats let out a hiss that had Domenic almost peeing his pants, and then as one group, the rats began running at him. Domenic took a step backwards and looked behind him quickly, seeing the rats there also running at him.

He had less than two seconds before they were on him...and he knew when they reached him it wouldn't be pleasant.

Domenic had always been an underachiever, though incredibly bright for a boy his age. Like many boys too smart for their age level, where other kids would work hard for the pride of getting A's, Domenic preferred to get C's or Ds and play video games all day. He had a quick tongue and never was without a wisecrack, and he always wanted to get in the last word on any argument with his folks or anyone else for that matter.

But despite his attitude about life and his lack of work ethics, he could think on his feet quickly and had the street smarts of a kid twice his age, and many other kids would have been envious if they knew Domenic's innermost thoughts.

So when the rats came at him, Domenic was already looking left and right, his mind a supercomputer, and he weighed any idea and dismissed it until he came up with one that would work.

One second after the rats charged, Domenic was already rush-ing to the left and the building there. He jumped up onto a wooden crate and then onto a trashcan, the metal lid snapping and bending under his weight.

He mentally thanked his luck it was a metal can and not a Rubbermaid one. The reason it wasn't was that rats could eat through the rubber containers easily with their sharp teeth, but at least the metal ones provided more of a challenge, though with determination the rodents could eat through metal and even stone given enough time.

Domenic's feet landed loudly on the metal lid, and as the can began to wobble, he jumped into the air, his hands catching the lowest rung on the rusting fire escape. The trashcan tipped over, garbage falling out, the rats lunging over it to reach the hanging boy.

He swung there, his sneakers in the air for almost a full three seconds before he began to pull himself up. Meanwhile, below him, the rats tried to jump up and bite him, some climbing onto the backs of their brethren and then lunging upwards, nipping at his heels with each jump. Each time they would twist in the air to fall back down to the ground.

Domenic had to use all his strength to do the one chin-up that allowed him to make it onto the next rung. As he did this, he silently thanked his gym teacher for making him do chin-ups in gym class, otherwise he doubted he would have had the upper body strength to pull himself up. As he climbed onto the fourth rung and looked down, the rats were swarming in circles, like black land sharks with feet and tails.

"Ha, ya missed me!" he laughed, his heart pounding a mile a minute.

One of the rats stopped and looked directly up at him, hissing, its whiskers twitching angrily. As Domenic stared into its beady eyes, he could have sworn it was actually thinking, actually trying to figure out how to get the boy that had escaped their teeth.

Flashlights lit up the night and every rat looked in the direction of the light, then they spun around and slinked off, gone in less than a second. Domenic watched them go, amazed at how fast they were.

He looked up as a pickup truck rolled down the alley. It was just someone using the alley to cut between streets, and the driver didn't know they had scared away giant rats, or see Domenic hanging from the fire escape.

Domenic watched the pickup's brake lights disappear at the end of the alley when it turned onto the street.

He stayed on the fire escape for a full hour after that, too scared to come down. But as he hung there, his hands wrapped around the metal rung, his feet on the bottom one, he watched people come and go. He saw cooks tossing out trash and more than half a dozen couples walking down the alley to cut through it like he'd been doing. He even saw a mugging, but it was quick and the mugger only had a knife and it seemed to Domenic that the two knew each other.

Finally, he decided it was safe to climb down, and with his heart in his throat, he dropped down, expecting the rats to come charging out of the shadows and this time finish the job they'd tried so hard to do.

When his feet touched the ground and nothing happened, he turned and ran as fast as his legs would carry him out of the alley and all the way home. He ran so fast he almost fell five times and only luck allowed him to keep his balance. It was as if his upper half wanted to go faster than his lower half, his legs not able to keep up. He knew if he'd been a cartoon character, his upper torso would have left his legs in the dust.

He made it home in record time but was already very, very late. As he ran up the front walk, he saw both his parents' cars parked in the driveway and all the lights were on in the house.

As he burst inside, his parents spun around, their faces filled with relief to see he was safe.

"Oh, thank God, Dom, I thought…I thought…" she began to cry as she ran to him and hugged him, squeezing so tightly he couldn't breathe.

"I'm fine, Mom, really, but you won't believe what happened to me."

His father walked over to him and hugged him, too, then said, "Do you have any idea what time it is? I've been calling you on your cell for over an hour. You're in big trouble, young man."

"No, wait, Dad, you don't understand, I was attacked on my way home. They almost got me but I managed to…" He told his story, not leaving anything out. By the time he'd finished, he and his parents were all sitting at the kitchen table, Domenic's dinner untouched before him as he animatedly told them what had happened.

When he was finally finished, he leaned back in his chair and looked at his mother and father, waiting to hear how amazed they were that he had outwitted the rats, how he had survived when other children hadn't, and how he could shed some light on what was happening in their small town.

Instead, his father leaned forward and said, "Wow, that's some story you made up and I swear if you put half that much energy into your school work, you'd be getting all A's. I'm not even going to dignify your story with a rebuttal but I can tell you what I am going to do. For losing your cell phone and coming home late and worrying your mother half to death, you're grounded for one week, no TV, no video games and right home after school. Do I make myself clear?"

Domenic merely blinked at his father, too shocked to believe what he'd just heard. His father's jaw was tight, his fists clenched and Domenic knew that look well. No matter what he said, or how he protested, neither his father, nor his mother would listen to him.

"Now get up to your room, take a shower and get to bed. And I don't want to hear any more nonsense about giant rats ever again." He turned to Domenic's mother and said, "Why do children think their parents are so damn stupid? Like we weren't kids once and did and said the exact same things to get out of breaking curfew or whatever. And why would he make up a story about giant rats when everyone knows it's a pack of dogs?"

"I don't know, dear. That boy, sometimes..." His mother nodded, entirely on her husband's side. Her initial fear of Domenic having gone missing was already forgotten and she was back in her role as disciplinarian.

"I agree with your father completely, Domenic. You were very irresponsible tonight and I have to tell you, I'm so disappointed in your actions. I thought you were better than this. And I'm truly hurt that you thought it was no big deal to lie to us."

"But I..." Domenic began, but then stopped, seeing this time he wouldn't be getting the last word in. With nothing else to be said, he slid off his chair and hobbled out of the room, his legs sore from his massive sprint home.

"Maybe it would have been better if the rats had gotten me, then you'd all see..." he mumbled wanting to get the last word in no matter what.

"What did you say, son? Do you have something to add? Do you want to try for two weeks grounded?"

"No, Dad, I didn't say anything," he said and left the room, his head hung low in frustration.

- 5 -

The next morning, the police were out in force, searching for Bobby Fisher and the killers of Zachery Jorgensen, Susan Mills and her baby.

The news channels were talking about it twenty-four/seven, and the public was warned to be on the lookout for wild dog packs.

That was still the story the authorities were going with and there was no one to say they were wrong.

Well, except for Domenic Salvatore, but he was punished and his parents didn't believe him anyway, assuming he had made up the tall tale to get out of being grounded.

Like most children, he was now being picked up and dropped off at school each day. Once home, he was banished to his bed-room, where all he had to do to keep busy was read, play with his toys or draw.

Without the internet, video games or television, truly his life was Hell on Earth, and he wondered if he would be able to survive the entire week of being grounded.

Domenic had always been a night owl, sometimes staying up as late as three in the morning, even though he had to be in school by eight.

It was three days into his punishment, a little after two in the morning, and he was looking out his window, bored, watching the trees sway with the light wind.

His parents were fast asleep in their bedroom and had been for hours. There was a half moon this night and with the help of the one street lamp, the area around his house was bathed in a pallid, gloom-filled light.

Shadows were everywhere and he felt a chill run down his spine.

Spooky, was the word that came to mind.

The street was entirely deserted, not a soul about. The houses surrounding his were all dark, not a single window with a glimmer of light peeking out of drawn curtains or shades.

He turned around to look at his television sitting on his cabinet in the corner of the room. The cable wire was missing, a clever ploy of his father to keep him from using it when his parents went to sleep.

The same for his game console. It was there, but the power cord was missing, thus making the three hundred dollar system nothing but a paperweight.

With a weary sigh, he turned back and gazed out the window, wondering if he should just go to bed and get it over with. Because he stayed up so late, he never got up easy. His mother had even taken to splashing him with a cupful of water on a few rare occasions, that added to the constant threats of: "Or else," and "So help me if you don't get up."

As he watched the dark street, he suddenly spotted movement to his left and his head naturally followed it.

Two sets of headlights were coming down the road, one in front of the other.

When they reached his house, Domenic saw two, nondescript white vans. They drove past his home and stopped two doors down in the middle of the street. The lights on both vehicles went out and he watched in surprise as men began to climb out of them; all were dressed in white hazmat suits, even their heads covered, the plastic faceplates steaming up as the person breathed.

A white tent was quickly set up over the single manhole cover, the tent blocking out their actions from view.

Domenic, ever curious, ran to his bureau and pulled out a set of binoculars from the bottom drawer. The binoculars were a remnant from two years ago, when he'd told his mother he had a passing fancy with watching birds outside his window.

It had been a casual utterance, not worth her notice, but the next day, always trying to get him into something more positive than video games, his father had run out and bought him the binoculars, hoping his son would become a birdwatcher.

Other than spying on his neighbors when he was bored, the binocs had never had a bird locked in its crosshairs.

After grabbing the binoculars, he dashed back to the window and put his eyes to them. At first the world was fuzzy, but he played with the center knob for a few seconds, and ever so slowly, the world began to take on clarity.

He found he was staring at a tree three houses down, so he shifted his gaze until he found the top of the white tent. Then, like a sniper adjusting to his prey, he lowered the binoculars until the tent was in full view.

By luck alone, the tent flap of the cloth structure was facing Domenic, and as he focused a little more and zoomed in, he found he had a bird's eye view of the interior.

The manhole cover was off and had been pushed to the side, and he saw the white-suited men climbing into the sewer. One man—he assumed it was a man—held something in his hand. It reminded Domenic of an old transistor radio.

He watched the tableaux for ten full minutes, until the men in the sewer climbed out and the tent was quickly taken down and packed away.

Domenic realized they were about to leave and his curiosity was so high that he couldn't just let them go without knowing more about what they were doing.

Within seconds, he had on his sneakers and jacket and was opening the window to his room and crawling out onto the roof. Below his room was the den to his home and it was easy for him to walk across it and climb down the small trellis mounted to the side of the house.

Landing softly in the grass, he ran to the backyard and grabbed his bicycle.

Less than a minute had passed since he'd decided to follow the men in white, and as he pedaled as hard as he could and returned to the street, he saw the brake lights of the second van turning the corner.

Pedaling even faster, he cut through the yard of the corner house, and when he got back onto the street, the brake lights were there again; that is until the van turned yet another corner.

Putting on as much speed as he was capable of, he once more swung around the corner to just catch the brake lights again. He was beginning to think this wouldn't last, that sooner or later the van would outdistance him, when the two vans had to stop at a traffic light.

That gave Domenic the edge he needed and he raced up to the rear of the second van and grabbed hold of the rear bumper with his left hand. When the traffic light changed from red to green, he was still attached to the vehicle and held on with only one hand on the handlebars as the driver swerved around potholes while following the lead van.

They traveled for ten minutes and then stopped once more in the middle of the street. Domenic let go and rode off to the side, riding right into a large copse of shrubs that bordered an abandoned building.

As he looked around to see where he was, he saw it was an area mostly deserted on the north edge of town. Another few minutes would have brought him into Melrose. The buildings around him were warehouses and only one or two houses could be seen, most looking like they'd been abandoned or were ill-maintained.

Once more, the tent was set up and the men in white climbed down into the sewer. Watching from afar, Domenic tried to imagine what the men were doing, but nothing came to mind. He began rifling through all the movies he'd seen in his eleven years on Earth but nothing made sense, not here, in the real world.

Fifteen minutes later, the last man had come up from the sewer and the team started packing everything up again.

As the vans began to drive away, Domenic shot out of the bushes and grabbed hold of the rear bumper of the second van again.

Staying in the blind spot of the driver, he held on for dear life as the van weaved its way through the city and finally stopped at the south edge of town, on the border of Melrose once more. Whatever these men were looking for, it seemed it was within the town limits of Wakefield.

The same dance was enacted, the men climbing out and setting up the tent over a manhole in the center of the road. A few late night motorists passed the tent, some curious, most not. Most just wanting to get home and get to bed.

The men went into the sewer while the others looked at equipment and talked amongst one another.

Domenic was hunched down behind a pair of trashcans, and watched with fascination. Thinking back to his narrow escape from the rats, he couldn't help but wonder if the men had anything to do with it. He studied their white suits, and even at his young age, he knew these people had to belong to some government or private agency. He didn't know what he'd found in these men, but he knew he'd found something big, something that could prove he wasn't lying about the rat attack.

And then, as if in answer to his questions, he saw a flurry of activity inside the tent. Men were moving around quickly, and he watched as one man ran to the rear of the first van, reached into the back, and pulled out a large metal cage.

When the man returned, the ones that had gone down into the sewer were returning.

Domenic watched in amazement as the last man came out of the opening, and passed up what was without a doubt a large black rat.

The rodent was either dead or asleep by the looks of it and it was placed inside the cage and rushed back to the rear of the van.

There was some slapping of shoulders and shaking of hands as the team began packing things up.

Fifteen minutes after arriving, the tent was back inside the van and the manhole was being returned to the opening to close it off once more. Domenic had a dilemma. Was he going to follow the vans or return home before he was caught for leaving his house? He knew if his father caught him sneaking out so late he would be in so much trouble that his previous grounding would be like a day at the beach, but he also remembered how his parents had looked and treated him when he'd told them about the rats.

He was a lot of things, but one thing he wasn't, was a liar. If he ever wanted to clear his name with his parents, he would need proof that the rats were real.

As the men got into the vans, Domenic made his decision and pedaled to the rear once again and held on, the vehicles pulling out.

He didn't know where they were going but he knew these people, whoever they were, knew something about the rats that had attacked him, and he wanted to know too.

- 6 -

While Domenic played detective, the rest of Wakefield slept.

In a two family house on Water Street, all wrapped up snuggly in their beds, was the Murphy family. The house was locked up tight, all the first floor windows closed and secured, just in case the roving pack of wild dogs was in the area.

Stan and Emily Murphy were in their bedroom, Stan snoring loudly as usual. Emily had taken a sleeping pill to help counteract her husband's snoring. He would deny it till the cows came home, telling her she was imagining it. One of these days, she planned on setting up the camcorder, so she would have irrefutable proof that she slept next to a chainsaw each night.

Down the hall was their daughter Emma's bedroom. Emma was eleven with brown hair that she usually wore in pigtails. She had wide trusting eyes and red cheeks that never seemed to lose their pinkness.

Hugging her teddy bear, she dreamed about being a singer one day and was excited for the talent contest at school in a few weeks. She sighed softly in her sleep, a smile creasing her lips as she dreamed of being famous, like Brittany Spears or Avril Lavigne.

She was in a good place right now.

The next door down from Emma's was baby Jenny's bedroom. Jenny was short for Jennifer and she was thirteen months old this night. Jenny was a happy baby, with bright blue eyes and blonde hair.

Tonight she wore a blue pajama one piece, and her favorite plush bunny rabbit was beside her. As she slept, a light scratching could be heard coming from outside the window facing the street.

It was open to let in the cool breeze. Her parents had left it open, not worrying about the dog attacks. After all, why would they? Dogs couldn't climb the side of a house.

But rats could.

A dozen rats, one at a time, each scurried up the drainpipe and onto the roof, then walked along it until they were directly over the window. As the others waited, the last rat slid down the cable wire next to the window and landed on the window sill. It took seconds for it to chew through the thin screen and enter the bedroom.

As it scurried into the hole, and its tail disappeared from sight, the other rats followed, each one gracefully sliding down the cable wire and into the bedroom.

They gathered in the center of the room and looked up at the crib and the sleeping baby within.

One hopped onto the crib by scurrying up a wooden leg and onto the headboard. From there it jumped onto the sailboat mobile hanging over the baby. It looked down at Jenny, its beady eyes taking in what wan light filtered into the room from the nightlight in the hallway. It flicked its whiskers in anticipation.

Downstairs, in the living room, Dusty, the Murphy's two year old German shepherd, perked his head up. Something had awakened him, only he didn't know what. His head flicked up and down, his nose twitching as a scent came to him. His ears flexed back and forth, turning slightly to catch the noise that had awakened him, and the hairs on the back of his head stood up.

Then, as if a bell had gone off, the dog jumped up and dashed to the stairs leading to the second floor, a low growl coming from his mouth.

Whatever he'd heard, it came from upstairs.

Taking the steps two at a time, Dusty first entered the parents' bedroom. The room was dark, only a sliver of light filtering in from the streetlamp on the sidewalk. Stan moaned softly in his sleep and rolled over, Emily shifting as well. Both fought for dominance over the blankets.

Dusty backed out of the bedroom, seeing that the noise didn't come from there.

Next he walked into Emma's room.

The room was dark as well and Emma was sleeping softly, her favorite bear wrapped tightly in her arms. Dusty sniffed a few times at the foot of the bed but didn't see anything amiss.

Then he heard it, the same sound that had woken him. Spinning quickly, he dashed out of the room, hitting the door open as he passed back into the hallway. He was almost galloping now, only the short length of the space to the next room slowing him down.

He charged into Jenny's room at full speed and then promptly stopped after passing through the doorway.

If a dog could be in shock, then Dusty was doing exactly that. He stared at the scene before him, blinking quickly. But as soon as he felt the surprise that greeted him come and go, he lowered his head and began to growl, his instincts kicking in to protect the family, and at this moment, that was baby Jenny.

Dusty continued to growl, and was about to let out a threatening bark when the rats before him attacked en masse. Three rodents came at the dog head-on, while three more swerved to the side to attack Dusty's right flank. Meanwhile, four more rats attacked Dusty's left flank, sliding across the floor, their black-furred bodies blending into the gloom permeating the room.

Dusty went into action as well, charging at the three rats coming straight for him. His mouth opened wide and he sank his teeth into the first rat he reached, his sharp incisors sinking into the rodent's black fur. The rat screeched in pain as it was practically bifurcated by the dog's sharp teeth, the small body going limp as its spine was snapped, the rest of its body following. Only bits of flesh and tendons kept the two pieces from completely falling away separately. Dusty spit out the carcass, the fetid taste of the rat's blood making him sick; his muzzle dripped crimson as he spun his head around to bite another rat.

Seven rats swarmed over him from both sides and he snapped and scratched them, trying to fend them off. He began to spin around in a circle, hoping to keep them at bay. One rat jumped onto the dog's back and sharp claws sank deep. Like a cowboy riding a bucking bronco, the dog tried to shake the rat and only when Dusty slammed his body against a wall did the rider break loose.

While Dusty fought for his life, the rat that had jumped onto the mobile over the crib dropped down next to Jenny, who had woken up and was crying from all the noise in her room.

The rat sniffed the baby three times, its whiskers twitching, then knowing the baby was the prey it wanted, it jumped onto Jenny's chest and sank its teeth into her neck. Jenny had time for one loud scream before her jugular was torn out, the rat feeding on the sweet young meat. It was so tender, so tasty, that the rat almost continued to feed, but then it stopped, knowing its orders were to bring back any meat found to the nest.

Reluctantly, the rodent stopped feeding on baby Jenny, who had already bled out. Grabbing the baby's arm in its teeth, the rat dragged the small corpse to the edge of the crib, where other rats had been chewing at the wooden poles that made up the side of the crib.

When enough had been eaten through, the baby was dragged out of the crib where it fell to the floor in a lump, a blood trail behind it.

Dusty was still battling for his life, but it was a battle he couldn't win. The odds simply weren't with him.

His rear legs were bleeding profusely, his sides had multiple slices, one ear was hanging by a thread of gristle, and one of his eyes had been slashed by a sharp claw so that now the socket leaked a milky white fluid.

Barking loudly, Dusty lunged for another rat, sinking his teeth into its side. The rat's screech almost sounded human as Dusty shook his head back and forth, the rat snapping to and fro. the teeth sinking in deeper. Finally, something important was punctured and the rat spasmed and went limp. Dusty opened his mouth to shake the carcass loose but his teeth were too far embedded into the flesh to get it out of his mouth, and without the use of his paws, it was all but impossible.

He jumped and kicked at the rats but they swarmed over him, biting, scratching and chewing into him. One rat was already burrowing into his side, tearing at the dog's insides an inch at a time.

Dusty let out one long, mournful wail and then succumbed to his wounds, slumping to the blood-covered bedroom floor. The rats covered the dog's body, making sure it was dead before breaking off the attack.

"What the hell? Jenny!" Stan Murphy yelled from the doorway, as he stood in abject horror at the scene before him. Behind him, Emily watched in astonishment, a scream already leaving her lips at the sight of the blood-soaked crib and the floor covered with rats half the size of the family dog, which was buried under black bodies and had been torn into bloody pieces.

Near the window, two rats were pulling baby Jenny's corpse through the hole in the screen. A thin trail of blood led from the crib to the window, showing where the baby had been dragged.

As Stan's gaze went to the window and the screen, he saw Jenny's limp legs sliding through, then blurred shapes.

"Call 9-1-1, Emily!" Stan yelled and ran into the bedroom, thinking he was going to reach the window, push the screen out, and save his child.

He made it halfway into the room before the first rats attacked him. Sharp incisors that could eat through metal and stone sank into Stan's leg and began to gnaw like a small saw. Stan yelped in pain and tried to kick the rodent off him, but as soon as he felt the stab of pain, more were on him. One scurried up his leg, its claws sinking into his flesh under his pajamas, and climbed right up to his shoulders. He tried to swat it away but it scooted to the other shoulder, balancing precariously. Others did the same until he had three rats on him, each one biting and scratching, drawing blood with each second that ticked by on the kitty cat clock with the big white eyes on the wall. The eyes on the clock flicked back and forth and each flick was one more wound on Stan's body.

It wasn't long before he tripped on a rat and fell face first into the pile of organs and gore that had been his faithful dog Dusty. Spitting out the viscous fluid, he tried to get up, but two rats lunged for his throat, each one tearing out pieces. One took his Adam's apple while another sliced into his jugular.

Gurgling his next scream, he was quickly covered with rodents who tore at him.

Only they didn't eat the meat, finding it distasteful, and instead spit it back out.

While Stan gave out his death rattle, Emily was running down the hallway to her bedroom, where she hoped to get inside and slam the door and call for help.

She didn't get far.

No more than halfway down the hall the first of the rats fell on her, nipping at her ankle and holding on tightly. With the added weight of the rodent attached to her foot, she lost her balance and fell, her nose hitting the hardwood floor hard enough to break it.

Prone and helpless, she rolled over and used her hands to fend off the attacking rats, only to have them sink their teeth in her arms and fingers. She screamed and kicked in pain as more came out of Jenny's bedroom, tracking bloody footprints as they went. Blood slid down Emily's face, her nose now askew.

And then Emily was covered in a carpet of black fur as they bit and clawed at her.

A few feet up the hallway, Emma opened her bedroom door, her eyes wide with fright at all the screaming and yelling going on. Though she was scared, at hearing her parents yelling she needed to see what was happening.

She stepped into the hallway just in time to watch her mother die.

Emily rolled over and tried to crawl away but the rats were too heavy on her back. She looked up, her face a mask of blood, to see Emma gazing at her in horror.

"Momma?" Emma squeaked as she stared, and took a step towards her when Emily let out one last shriek, "No, get back to your room! Don't let them get you!"

A rat pounced on Emily's head and sank its teeth into the back of her neck, killing her instantly as it burrowed into her brainstem. Emily's head fell forward, bounced once and lay still.

Emma hadn't moved, only stared at her mother as the rats swarmed over her. It wasn't real, it couldn't be. She was dreaming. She was having a bad nightmare.

She shifted her left foot and a floorboard below her creaked. Sounding loud in the hallway, all the rats on her mother looked up as one, their bloody whiskers flicking, their eyes boring into Emma as if they could read her mind.

Emma still didn't move; she was frozen in shock.

Anthony Giangregorio

Then the first rat jumped off Emily and ran at Emma, its front and back legs moving in rhythm, the rodent almost galloping. As the lead rat ran for the young meat, the rest followed, sliding off Emily's corpse like a black cloak. They ran down the hallway, bustling to be the first to take down the little girl.

At the very last second, Emma snapped out of it and took a step backwards, then another, and another. As the first rat lunged at her, she screamed and kicked out, catching the rodent in the face and knocking it back into its brethren.

She turned and dashed for her bedroom, a swirling mass of hungry black rats on her tail.

- 7 -

Domenic's hand was killing him as he held onto the rear bumper of the van. Three times he'd almost lost control of his bicycle but had managed to regain control at the last second. Looking down, the ground rushed by, and he swallowed the knot in his throat.

He didn't want to think what would happen to him if he fell. A broken bone if he was lucky. A broken neck if he was unlucky, plus half his skin rubbed off as he slid along the pavement.

The van he was attached to had reached speeds of forty miles an hour. Not such a big deal inside the vehicle, but when you were hanging onto the van and riding a bicycle, well, things became a lot more dangerous.

The ride lasted a little over twenty minutes and Domenic waited to be discovered, but no one spotted him. He did get a few odd looks from other motorists, who passed him with curiosity.

But no one did anything such as spinning to race after the van so they could warn the van driver.

Thank God for apathetic people that minded their own business, Domenic thought.

The van turned onto a road in desperate need of repair and Domenic found himself struggling to stay upright. The front tire of his bicycle was bouncing back and forth and the only reason he hadn't fallen down yet was because the van had to slow down to get through the potholes.

Then his tire hit one pothole that it couldn't handle and he suddenly realized he was flying through the air. He landed hard but rolled with it, and other than a sore arm and a scratched knee and elbow, he'd come through the fall intact.

His bike fell also, rolling end over end to land a few feet from him. The front tire still spun slowly.

He wasn't spotted by either van, thanks to all the streetlamps in the area not working. Or perhaps they had been turned off

Quickly getting to his feet, he grabbed his bike and hopped on it, wincing from his sore extremities. He began pedaling, slowly at first, but as he worked the kinks out of his limbs, he was soon pedaling faster.

The vans had gotten a good head start on him, and if it wasn't for them going slow to ride over the potholes, he would have lost them this time.

Careful not to take another spill, he rode on the edge of the street, partially in the gutter to avoid the worst of the holes. By doing this, he began to gain ground on the vans.

Swinging around a corner at full speed, he was almost discovered when he saw a large tractor trailer parked before him, both vans pulling up and stopping at the rear of the semi. Acting fast, Domenic turned to the left and drove straight into a copse of bushes and trees in need of a good pruning.

Letting his bike fall to the high grass, he peered out of the bush he was in to see if he'd been spotted.

As he watched the vans, he saw two men walk around the semi. Both held flashlights and looked like some sort of security by the way they acted. Both men were dressed in black suits, reminding Domenic of G-men.

He saw the green street sign at the corner, and with the wan light from the moon, he read the white letters: **Commercial St.**

Looking around the area some more, he saw there was nothing but one and two story buildings, and large open lots. The street sign said it all. He was in a commercial district, which meant this late at night it would be deserted.

The rear of the semi began to open, exposing a well-lit interior. Domenic could see it looked a lot like a laboratory. Within the trailer were computers, test tubes and other assorted items, plus people were walking around holding clipboards and were wearing white lab coats. Domenic thought they looked like the one his teacher wore in science class.

As the door came to a stop on the ground, it became a ramp for the people to access the inside.

Domenic watched as the men in white from the vans began to off-load the vehicles, two men carrying the cage with the large rat in it. The rat was hissing and scratching at the cage, trying to either escape or attack the men carrying it.

All personnel entered the semi and the door began to close again.

The sound of hydraulics filled the night until the door sealed closed with the hiss of air.

From the bushes nearby, Domenic bit his lip, knowing he had to get inside that semi. Everything he wanted to know was in that rolling laboratory.

The trick would be how to get inside without being discovered.

- 8 -

Rats were nipping at Emma's heels as she dashed for her bedroom. A chill went down her spine with the expectation of feeling a bite on one of her legs.

But though the rats were fast, she was faster.

Running full tilt into her bedroom, she spun around and began shutting the door, only to have it stop three inches from closing.

She pushed again and something springy stopped it from slamming shut.

Looking down, she saw that she'd trapped a rat between the door and its jamb. The rodent was screeching terribly as the door crushed its insides, the rat's eyes seeming to pop out of its head, its tongue hanging out.

Behind it, others were trying to force their heads through the opening, and Emma knew if she let up on the door for even a second, the weight of the rodents would force it open. If that happened, she had no doubt what her fate would be.

The rat at her feet hissed and snapped at her and she had to move her left leg back or risk being scratched by the trapped creature.

Knowing she had no choice, she let out a cry filled with anguish, terror and pain, and began pushing on the door as hard as she could.

It felt like there was a ripe orange in the door, blocking it, the squishiness continuing. The more she pushed, the more the door began to inch closed.

The rat was screeching to the point it almost sounded human. Its eyes were bulging from their sockets even more, its tongue flopping back and forth as the rodent was slowly cut in half by the dull edge of the door.

For any animal it would have been an excruciating way to die, but on top of it being bifurcated, the rats behind it were clawing and trying to climb over it, wanting to get inside the bedroom and the young meat within.

Emma was crying, long loud sobs that shook her small frame. Her vision was blurry from tears, phlegm running down over her lips to hang from her chin.

She had never been so terrified in her young life, and though a strong girl, even her iron will was giving out by the sheer unimaginable scenario she now found herself in.

With a mighty yell she let the door bounce back two inches, and with as much force as she could muster, she used her shoulder and shoved the door closed.

The rat at her feet couldn't take the pressure, and with a loud *pop*, the front and rear ends of the creature separated, the front end shooting through the gap to land three feet from the door inside the room.

The resistance to the bedroom door gone, Emma slammed it closed with a loud bang. No sooner did it close than the sounds of scratching came to her, as well as more screeching.

She turned to see the severed rat was still alive, only three inches behind its front legs there was nothing but a pool of blood and hanging entrails.

The size of a very large housecat, the rat hissed and shrieked so loud that Emma had to cover her ears or go mad.

She squeezed her eyes closed, and would have kept them like that, but she heard the unmistakable sound of claws on the hardwood floor. She knew that sound well from her dog, Dusty. When he padded around the house, his claws would click-clack.

Opening them, the half-a-rat was crawling towards her, its mouth open wide, its half a tongue lolling to the left lazily—it had bit off the rest when it had been cut in two. Bloody spittle dripped from its mouth, and as it crawled, it left behind blood and pieces of itself. In the gloom of her bedroom, Emma could see the bits and pieces glistening, catching what light was available.

She turned and promptly threw up, the warm spray splashing her feet and the throw carpet in the center of the floor.

The rat howled as it crawled at her, a sound reminiscent of a cat worfing up a large hairball; a warbling in its throat that bespoke how much pain it was truly in. But despite the agony the rodent suffered, it still hunted Emma, and she knew as she watched it come for her, that it wouldn't stop until she killed it…or it killed her.

Her eyes darted about the room, looking for something she could use as a weapon, and finally rested upon a statue of a unicorn. It was on a small table on the opposite side of the room. It was heavy, she knew this well when she'd had to move it one time to clean behind the table. It was a gift from her Aunt Ruth for her ninth birthday. A few years ago she'd been obsessed with unicorns and more than ninety percent of her room had been filled with toys, posters, clothing and other items with unicorns on them.

Since then, she'd grown out of unicorns and had gotten rid of most of her collection, but the statue was still special in her heart because her aunt had given it to her.

But now, as she looked at the statue, all she saw was a weapon to save her life.

As the rat got within two feet of her, she swallowed the scream rising in her throat and jumped over the rodent.

Her feet went over it by only a few inches and the rat tried to scratch her, its head following the prey as she flew over its head.

Then she was down and across the room, the rat spinning around, its intestines dragging behind it like shiny red worms.

The bedroom door was shaking, the rodents trying their best to get inside. Near the bottom of the door the wood was flexing and the first signs of a claw could be seen, the first rat digging through the door.

Emma didn't see this; she was too focused on the rat before her. The half-a-rat had spun around and was crawling over its bloody back trail, hissing, screeching and warbling; refusing to die.

Emma grabbed the statue and held it over her head, the rat moving closer with each second. Her arms began to shake as she supported the unicorn and she knew she was about to drop it.

The rat crawled closer, no more than a foot away from her. Emma looked down at it, the rat looking up at her. Its beady eyes locked with hers and for one instant, rodent and human saw each other...truly saw each other as two separate entities.

Then Emma brought the statue down onto the half-a-rat, squashing it flat.

The unicorn landed heavily, and the eyes on the half-a-rat popped out of their sockets to hang by bits of sinew and optic nerve. She felt another bout of vomiting coming, but before she could begin the first heave, the bottom of the bedroom door began to break apart and first one, then more rats poured through the hole.

She screamed and ran for the bathroom connected to her bedroom.

Once more she reached it and slammed the door as the first rat hit it, shaking the cheap wood in its frame.

She fell back and sat on the cold tile floor, staring at the door.

The scratching was more intense this time, as if the rats were upset that one of their kind had been killed and they were now seeking vengeance. Emma sat on the floor, crying, yelling for the rodents to go away, but of course, they wouldn't leave, not until they had her in their claws and tasted her sweet young flesh.

"Go away! Leave me alone! Mommy, help me!" she cried, sobbing so hard she could barely talk. She was so scared, more terrified than anytime in her life.

And then the first face began to appear as it chewed away at the door. A black, moist nose popped through, then teeth, then whiskers as the rat ate at the door as if it was nothing more than cardboard. Which wasn't far from the case. The door was a cheap fabricated barrier with a mostly hollow center and only real wood for the outside edges. Corrugated cardboard filled the interior.

"No, stop it! Go away!" she screamed but the rat ignored her pleas. It kept eating at the door until its entire head was visible. Seconds was all it needed to slip through the door, the rest of the pack right behind it.

Emma got to her knees, figuring she would retreat into the bathtub, when her hand hit a can of her mother's hairspray that had been on the edge of the vanity.

The can fell off and landed at her feet.

Desperate, not knowing if it would work, she picked it up and ran at the bathroom door and the rat's head still chewing at it. She went to all fours and sprayed the rat in the eyes with the hairspray, hitting it right between its dark orbs. The rat stopped chewing and let out a scream that rivaled the half-a-rat before it had been crushed.

It began to go crazy, trying to either go through the door or back out of the hole but it was stuck. Emma saw it wouldn't be stuck for long and her eyes began to search the bathroom for something else to use as a weapon. Her eyes fell on a nail file on a shelf to her right. Not understanding where her courage was coming from within her but not complaining, she grabbed the file and used it like a small blade, stabbing the head of the rat again and again. The rodent already blinded by the hairspray, Emma finished the job by taking out both its eyes, leaving bloody holes that seeped clear liquid as the rat spasmed.

Stabbing with her eyes closed, she finally hit paydirt when the blade slid into one of the open sockets and punctured the small brain, killing the rodent instantly. The rat went limp and she let out the breath she was holding, hoping she was safe now, that the rest of the pack couldn't get at her. But her relief was short-lived when the dead rat began to move again.

She shrieked in horror, not understanding what was going on. It was bad enough they were so big, but the rats still kept coming even after they were dead? It was too much.

What she didn't know was that the rat *was* truly dead, and its brethren were even now chewing at it, gnawing on its remains so they could get at the hole. Two more were starting new holes as well, on either side of the dead rat.

Suddenly, the dead rat was yanked back and another black furry face replaced it. Emma was ready and she sprayed the face right in the eyes with the hairspray, then began to stab it repeatedly.

To the right of the rat that had just been stabbed a new hole appeared, but before the rat could open it more than a few inches, it was stabbed in the mouth with the nail file.

Emma kept this up for over ten minutes, on her knees, spraying and stabbing repeatedly. Each time a rat was hit, it retreated to be replaced by a fresh one. It was almost like a game of whack-a-mole only with rats, hairspray and a stabbing file.

She was beginning to wonder if it would go on forever when suddenly the rats were gone from the door. As she stared at the bottom of the door with her weapons held before her, she waited for another face to appear but there was none.

Minutes passed and she waited but still no rats appeared. Slowly, her heart calmed and she began to feel tired as adrenalin left her system. A full half hour passed before she decided to take a peek through the hole to see what was going on in her bedroom.

Careful not to get too close to the hole, she lowered her head and peered out, seeing no movement at all.

She waited for a full five minutes, then took a chance and slowly, ever so slowly, reached up and opened the bathroom door, fully ready to slam it closed if she needed to.

The door cracked open to expose her bedroom, one devoid of all life. Her eyes went to the statue to see it had been shifted and the half-a-rat she'd killed was missing, only its blood remaining.

Careful not to step in any blood, she tip-toed out of the bathroom to her bedroom door. Once more she went to her knees and peered out of the hole on the bottom of the door, where tufts of black fur were stuck to the shredded wood.

The hallway was silent, nothing stirred.

Opening this door, too, she poked her head into the hallway and immediately began to cry at the sight of her mother lying dead on the floor.

No rats were seen so she ran out and to her mother, falling beside her and cradling her head. Her mother's eyes were open but she could see nothing, the body already cooling.

Emma sat with her for fifteen minutes and then gathered the will to go into Jenny's room. Standing at the doorway, she saw Dusty's mangled carcass and her father's body in a large pool of blood. There was no sign of Jenny or any of the dead rats that Dusty had killed. Unknown to Emma, the rats had taken their dead with them.

She checked her father but by now she was so numb she barely felt any new grief, her emotions were so overloaded. She was full. But still she cried. Through tears so thick she could barely see, she went to the phone in her parents' bedroom and made the call to the police.

She didn't hear the voice on the end of the line tell her help was on the way. She slumped down beside the bed, placed her face in her hands, and continued to cry.

- 9 -

There were two guards on duty walking around the semi, both wearing black, and both had bulges under their jackets. Domenic had seen enough movies to know what those bulges meant.

The men would walk around the truck then stop and talk for ten seconds or so, before they continued walking again. Domenic watched them do this five times until he had the rhythm of the men.

He prepared to make his move.

He wondered why he wasn't scared and figured it was from all those hours of playing violent video games. He smiled inwardly, wishing one of those know-it-all doctors from magazines who condemned the games could see him now. He bet it would make the guy's day.

The guards did their route, talked for a few moments, then walked away. There was a brief few seconds when both men were at opposite ends of the vehicle, and thus the middle of the semi was out of their line of sight.

Domenic waited for the 'sweet spot,' and when he saw it, he dashed out of the bushes he was hiding in and ran right for the underside of the semi. He made it just as both men rounded the vehicle and made eye contact with one another. They walked over to each other and talked for fifteen seconds—they were changing it up a bit—then continued their patrol.

Trying to control his breathing, Domenic watched the guard's feet as they moved away to make their circular route. Where he was hidden, he was completely hidden in the darkness, and could hear people walking above him inside the trailer. And if he listened hard enough, he could hear voices as well, not to mention the hum of a generator on the roof of the semi.

He began inching his way under the truck, looking up at its undercarriage. He didn't know what he was looking for so he searched for anything that might help him.

Each time the guards passed him, he ducked closer to the large tires. It was after he had made it to one end and then the other, and was on his way back to check the undercarriage for the second time, about ready to give up, that he spotted what looked like a hatch, complete with hinges.

Getting up close to it, so he was almost standing up, he studied the seam with his eyes.

Was there light coming through the crack? Or was it just his imagination?

Reaching up, he felt around the crack until he found what he believed to be a latch. He weighed his options.

He could leave now before anyone had seen him, go home and pretend he'd never gone out tonight. Or he could see if the hatch was unlocked and if so, open it. What would happen after that was anyone's guess.

More muffled voices and footsteps came from overhead and he decided he had to know what was going in the trailer. So with a silent prayer that he wasn't about to get caught, he tried the latch, more than a bit surprised when it popped open easily and the hatch swung down, swinging back and forth on its long hinge that went down one side of the door, reminiscent of a piano hinge.

Bright light immediately spilled down, hitting him square in the eyes. He had to blink and squeeze his eyes closed and then open them slowly to adjust his vision to the sudden brightness. When he could see better, he reached up and poked his head into the opening.

As he did this he imagined his head coming up in the center of the rolling lab and how he would look up and have people staring at him in surprise, wondering what a boy was doing there.

But as he peeked inside the lab, he found the hatch was below a stainless steel table, and before him were the feet and legs of the people he'd seen go inside.

He could hear them talking, and as he looked between a set of legs, he saw a reflection in a steel cabinet behind them. By watching the reflection, he could see what the people were looking at.

On the table, the giant rat they'd captured in the sewer lay unmoving. Its eyes were closed and Domenic wondered if it was alive or dead. Then he saw its side move as it inhaled and exhaled and he realized it was sleeping or unconscious. Three people that looked a lot like lab techs were poking and prodding it, taking blood and hair samples to then scurry away much like the specimen they were taking samples from.

From the rear of the rolling lab, two men appeared. The first had gray hair and was in his late sixties. He wore the typical lab coat denoting that he was a doctor of some kind, complete with wire-rimmed glasses and a pocket pouch on his breast pocket. The second man was in his forties and wore a black suit with polished black shoes. Though it was dark out, he wore sunglasses, and his hair was cut so short its brown color could barely be seen.

"Look, Dr. Saunders," the man in black said. "I don't want any excuses. This has already gotten way out of hand. It's escalated and people are dying out there. This needs to be resolved '*yester-day*,' before the public figures out that we've been lying to them for months."

The doctor was nodding vigorously. "Yes, yes, Mr. Connors, I understand completely and as soon as the nest has been found we can eradicate the rats, but until it's discovered, my hands are tied."

"That's not the answer I was looking for, Doctor," Connors said, his jaw taut as he ground his teeth in annoyance. He had a dislike for eggheads and Saunders was the eggiest. "What I want to know is why the rats are so damn big and how do we kill them."

"I will try my best to answer some of your concerns," Dr. Saunders said. "Please, come over here and let me show you the specimen we found tonight. It's really quite fascinating."

The two men walked through the lab until they were standing before the table with the sleeping rat. Under the table, Domenic shrank back a little, scared he'd be seen. Connors' voice sounded hard, like a man who would not take kindly to finding out a child had infiltrated the rolling lab.

Dr. Saunders began pointing at the rat and nodding as he spoke. "This is *Rattus rattus*, or more commonly known as the Black rat...or Ship rat, as well as Roof rat. Now, as you can see, this specimen is much larger than its normal counterparts you are familiar with, and thus far we haven't been able to figure out why this is. The teeth and ears are bigger, too, but only in proportion to the size of the body. Now, the Black rat is a very capable creature. It can scale walls and leap from rooftop to rooftop with ease to find food, and from reports coming in that is exactly what they are doing.

"As you know, about two months ago, an animal rights group broke into one of our testing labs and set all the animals loose. We were able to recover many of them but all the Black rats managed to escape into the sewers. I believe these are the offspring of those rats."

"How do you know that for sure?" Connors asked.

"Well, we don't know absolutely, but as you can see, this one has no tag on its ear, so one must assume given the three week gestation period of a female that this rat is its offspring. Many of the rats that escaped were mature male and females so given the time they have been free, one must assume that…"

"Okay, fine, it's an offspring," Connors said, wanting to keep the ball rolling. "What else?"

"Well, assuming they have been breeding, and no reason to think they are not, and given the time and how many escaped, as well as litters of five to ten at a time, we could have a nest of upwards of over two hundred rats with more each week."

"My God, are you serious?" Connors asked, his eyes wide. "These things are huge and if there's more of them they'll overrun the town in no time."

"Quite right, and that is why I think it's time to inform the public," the doctor said. "Before this gets out of hand. We don't want a repeat of the Middle Ages now, do we?"

Connors slammed his hand on the table so hard the sleeping rat moved slightly. "No. Out of the question. This has to remain quiet until we can eradicate them. So far the news media has been silenced with threats of National Security and anyone who knows the truth has been threatened with the Patriot Act. Wild dog attacks should be enough to keep people inside. For those stupid enough to ignore the warnings, we…" He changed topics. "Once we find the nest we can kill them and this whole mess can go away."

Dr. Saunders nodded as if he was speaking to a child. "Ah, but that's the problem. We have no idea of their behavior patterns or where they have nested. There are miles of sewers under the city, they could be anywhere. And then there's the subject of their choice of food."

"Explain," Connors said.

"Well, it's entirely an assumption at this point, mind you, but after the first few attacks, it appears the rats have taken on a taste for prepubescent meat."

"In English, Doctor."

"They are only eating human children, Mr. Connors. Our children are the ones they are eating. After looking over the data from the earlier attacks, the adults were killed but not eaten, the wounds are only enough to kill them. But the children have been taken, which means…"

"Jesus, they're hunting our kids?"

Dr. Saunders nodded. "I'm afraid so. Normally the Black Rat will feed on anything it can find from fruit and nuts to meat, but something has mutated them so that they only want to feed on our children." He shrugged. "In a way it's fortunate."

Connors blinked at the man. "How the hell could this be a good thing?"

He shrugged. "Well, at least they don't want to eat us adults."

- 10 -

Domenic couldn't believe what Saunders had said, but when he thought back to his attack in the alley, it all made sense. What he found hard to wrap his head around was the fact that people who were in charge, people his parents said he was supposed to trust, actually knew about the rats and yet were doing nothing to protect everyone.

Domenic was a little too young to entirely understand conspiracies and cover-ups, though he had an idea as a typical child living in the United States.

Dr. Saunders and Connors were still talking, but Domenic had heard enough. Slowly backing down, he let the hatch close over his head.

Backing away from beneath the semi, his head was swimming with what he'd heard. The rats were hunting children and the people that knew about it didn't care; their secrecy was more important to them. He was so caught up in trying to rationalize what he'd heard that he grew sloppy and didn't pay attention to where the two guards were located around the semi.

Popping up near the front of the trailer, he stood upright—about to sprint away—but instead found himself standing before one of the men.

"Hey, kid, what the hell are you doing here?" the guard asked, already reaching for his two-way radio.

Domenic said nothing, for a brief moment paralyzed by fear as the guard looked down on him. He could see the handgun in a shoulder holster under the man's jacket when it opened slightly from an errant breeze. The image of the man taking him somewhere and killing him, thus solving the problem of who he was and what he knew, filled his head.

"Come here," the guard demanded and reached down and grabbed Domenic by his upper arms. Before Domenic could move, he found himself being picked up, his legs dangling in the air.

And that's when he snapped out of his terror at being found and began to struggle. His legs began to swing back and forth even more, and he looked like a small child letting loose with a tantrum.

By sheer luck, one of his kicking feet accidentally struck the man in the groin, crushing one of his testacles and sending the other one up into his stomach.

One second the man's eyes were filled with anger at finding Domenic, then they were popping out of his head as intense agony filled his nether-regions.

Domenic suddenly found himself falling as the guard let him go and both landed heavily on the ground.

Domenic landed hard but he was young, so he bent his knees and rolled; meanwhile, the guard was wheezing, his face red. Domenic didn't even know what he'd done and wasn't about to stick around and ask, for as he got to his knees, he turned to see the other guard running at him with his weapon drawn.

Then an alarm began to sound, and suddenly the dark night was banished as spotlights rigged to the roof of the semi snapped on. Like the circle of light cast on an abductee in an alien movie, Domenic found himself exposed and scared out of his mind.

The rear door of the rolling lab began to descend and more men with guns began running out, each calling out to one another to their location. Domenic saw Connors in the group as well. The man didn't look very pleased.

A hand wrapped around Domenic's left ankle and he looked down to see the guard he'd kicked in the nuts lying prone, but with his hand on Domenic's leg. "You're not going anywhere, you little bastard," the man hissed, and Domenic could see it was hard for the man to talk.

Jumping backwards, he broke free of the guard's grip, and as the second guard came at him, hands outstretched to grab him, Domenic ducked and weaved, the man too slow for the quickness of youth.

Spinning on his right heel, Domenic took off running, his arms pumping like a locomotive, his legs a blur.

The men followed close behind, yelling and calling out to one another to where the intruder was. Domenic risked a glance over his shoulder to see the men were splitting up, some trying to flank him. He put on more speed and ran faster, reaching his bike in seconds and hopping on it. For a second he thought the chain on his bike was stuck in the bush but then he ripped it free and was on it, pedaling as fast as he could.

One guard was close, only a few feet away, and before Domenic could get up enough speed, he felt a hand on his back, trying to grab him.

His spine tingled and he felt like he had to pee as he focused on pedaling. Then the hand was on his jacket and he felt it tearing as he also felt himself being held back.

But then the material tore free and he shot forward, the guard left standing with a piece of Domenic's jacket in his hand. The ripping jacket caused the man to lose his balance as he ran, and he fell head first onto the pavement. His nose was flattened and blood gushed out to bathe the ground in red. Domenic saw none of this, concentrating on escaping. He didn't want to think what they would do to him, hell, what his parents would do to him if he was caught out in the middle of the night like this.

Domenic turned the corner and was on the next street a moment later, but the sounds of vehicles behind him, engines revving, came to him.

A half-second later, headlights lit up the night behind him and he swerved onto the sidewalk. Risking a glance over his shoulder, he saw two black SUV's barreling down the road like rolling dinosaurs. He could almost imagine the engines growling, hungering to feed on him.

The vehicles quickly closed the gap between hunter and prey, and when Domenic took another desperate look over his shoulder, he knew they would catch him in seconds…unless he did something they wouldn't expect.

As he looked around, he saw he'd left Commercial St. behind and was slowly coming into a neighborhood, complete with houses, driveways, and best of all—backyards.

It was dark again, the spotlights of the semi long gone but the SUV's had their high beams on, piercing Domenic's back with their brilliance. They had him locked on target and it was only a matter of time before he was caught.

One SUV surged forward, leaving the second to cover the rear. Domenic looked to his right to see the large vehicle coming up on him, until he was side by side with it. The passenger side, dark-tinted window went down and a man with a determined face was revealed. He held something that looked like a gun but wasn't. Domenic had seen enough movies to figure if it didn't shoot bullets, it had to be either a taser or a tranquilizer gun. Either one didn't work for him.

Domenic pedaled faster, trying to outdistance the V-8 engine SUV. He didn't understand how futile it was.

The man in the passenger seat leveled the gun at Domenic, prepared to end the chase right there, but before he could shoot, Domenic reached a corner. He took the corner sharp, almost hitting a light post as his back tire skidded on the sidewalk. Above his head, hanging from the phone line, he saw a pair of sneakers swaying in the night breeze, then he was past them.

For just a moment, the SUV wasn't near him, but an instant later it roared around the corner with squealing tires.

Unfortunately for the driver, there was a car double parked in the street. As the SUV raced around the corner and the driver tried to straighten the wheel, he found himself driving right into the back of the parked car.

Behind him, Domenic heard the tires squeal as brakes were applied, then the crunching of metal meeting metal in an embrace that would leave the parked car the loser but would also slow the SUV enough for Domenic to gain a considerable lead.

As the SUV came to a rocking halt, the trailing vehicle raced past it, this driver taking the corner slower and managing to avoid rear-ending the lead SUV, which was hissing steam from under the dented hood and leaking antifreeze.

Domenic glanced over his shoulder to see the chase was far from over.

He was now smack dab in a typical suburban neighborhood and his eyes were already searching for what he knew would be his only escape.

So far, the homes he passed had tall fences made of wood and plastic, but then, just as the second SUV began gaining on him, he saw what he wanted.

A home with an open front yard, flower beds, and best of all, no fences leading into the backyard.

As the passenger window of the second SUV began to roll down and another man leveled a similar-looking gun, Domenic veered to the right and into the front yard of the house. He felt something zip by his head and would never know how close he'd come to being shot with a tranquilizer dart. Then he was fighting for control of his bicycle as the tires bounced over the uneven lawn.

Behind him he heard the SUV slam to a halt with squealing tires and then four doors opening and closing, the *thud-thuds*, of the doors echoing in the still night.

Domenic rode into the backyard and almost drove right into an in-ground pool still not covered for the winter. At the last second he swerved and balanced on the lip, then was past it and in the back end of the yard. There was a six foot fence but the studs and framing was on his side. He quickly jumped off his bike, tossed it over the fence with everything he had—the back tire hung up on the top of the fence but he managed to shove it over, the bike landing rudely on the opposite side.

Then he was climbing, as agile as a monkey, and soon was dropping down on the other side. Picking up his bike, he rolled it away through the backyard and out onto the next street. Behind him he could hear voices, a splash, then more raised voices as one of the men fell into the pool. A second later, lights came on in the yard as the homeowners came to investigate who was taking a dip in the middle of the night in October.

Entering the next yard, Domenic kept going. This home had bushes separating the neighbor's property and it was easy for him to simply push his bicycle through the branches. He was on the next street over now and still he continued.

By the fourth street, he hunkered down and waited, only his pounding heartbeat in his ears to keep him company. Time went by and there was nothing moving, and as he calmed down, his eyes began to droop, the fading adrenalin rush leaving him exhausted.

He was hiding in the front bushes of a Victorian house with painted shutters and a lawn gnome on the front lawn. He was a few feet from the gnome, and as he stared at it, he kept waiting for it to get up and walk over to him, to then ask him what he thought he was doing in his owner's shrubbery in the wee hours of the morning. Of course it didn't move; it was a statue after all.

Only fifteen minutes had passed, but to him if felt like over an hour, and when he was about to come out of hiding and make his way home, a black SUV drove by, the same one that had been following him.

It went by slowly, the driver and passenger each holding high-powered flashlights that they aimed into the yards of the homes they passed. Domenic hunkered down when they rolled by his hiding spot, and other than the light hesitating on the gnome for a moment, the vehicle kept on moving, the low rumbling of the engine vibrating right up into his legs through the ground.

He waited another ten minutes and decided it was now or never. He could see the sun was just starting to come up, and though he didn't know what time it was, he knew it was coming on morning.

He went in the opposite direction of the SUV. At first he thought he was lost, but as he rode for a while, he came upon the Malden fire station that he recognized from the times he'd visited his grandmother with his mother. He knew if he got on Main Street, it would take him all the way into Melrose, and if he stayed on the same road, he would then end up in Wakefield.

Knowing where he was, he began to pedal faster, and in no time was on his way home.

He never saw the one rat that watched him from a sewer grating as he zipped by it when he passed from Melrose into Wakefield. The rat let him go, as the boy was moving too fast, and by the time it and its brethren would have tried to attack, the boy would have been long gone.

The sun was just kissing the horizon when Domenic pulled into the front yard of his home. He climbed up the side of his house and into his bedroom. After kicking off his shoes out of habit, he fell onto his bed in exhaustion, staring up at the ceiling.

His mind raced with everything that had happened, and now that he was safe in his bed, he couldn't help but wonder if it had all been a dream.

As he slowly pulled off his jacket and shirt and saw the large tear where he'd been grabbed, he knew it wasn't a dream at all, that it was all true.

Giant rats were in his town, hunting children and eating them, and the people that knew about it didn't care, and were only worried about keeping it quiet.

He was in danger of being attacked—or worse—again, and so were all of his friends. He had to do something about it.

The question was: what could an eleven year old kid do about giant rats and conspiracies?

- 11 -

"Domenic, it's seven thirty; it's time to get up," his mother said from his bedroom door. "Come on or you're going to be late…again."

He ignored her and dove deeper into the covers.

Sighing heavily, she walked into the bedroom and opened the shade, bright sunlight shining in.

"Did you hear me? I said it's time to get up." She was picking up his clothes, something she did far too often. But no matter how much she nagged him, Domenic never listened.

"Just five more minutes," Domenic groaned from under his pillow. He'd fallen asleep a little after five that morning and the only two hours rest wasn't working for him at all. Now that he thought about it, he should have tried to stay up, but after he'd calmed down he was so tired he couldn't help but fall asleep.

"No, there's no time. I'll be driving you this morning, too."

Though he could barely open his eyes, that made him curious. His mother never drove him unless it was pouring rain or there was so much snow on the ground that he would have to walk in the street. She didn't want him to get hit by a car so she'd drive him. Anything else and he would walk. It wasn't so bad if it was nice out. The school was about twenty minutes away if he walked slow…and he was a slow walker, always had been; also usually dragging his heels to the point he wore the sneakers out in a few months.

"Why are you gonna drive me?" he asked, his voice muffled from under the covers.

She sat on his bed and slowly pulled back the covers and pillow. He groaned again and turned to the side, wanting to fall back to sleep more than anything.

"I'm driving you because there was another dog attack last night. The Murphy's from two streets over. They were attacked in their home. From what the news said, only their daughter Emma survived. It's terrible."

That woke him and he sat straight up, adrenalin filling his body as if his blood had been switched with the stuff. He knew Emma; they went to the same school. He thought she was cute, though he'd never told anyone.

"Is she all right?" he asked, thinking about the rats and knowing the wild dogs were made up.

His mother assumed he was just scared and she brushed the hair from his eyes and nodded. "Yes, from what I heard she's fine, though traumatized. Both her parents and her baby sister were killed in the attack. It's so horrible, I can't even imagine it."

Before Domenic considered his words, he began to blurt out what he knew about the rats, telling her again how he was attacked.

"Now, Dom, I thought we'd been through this with your father last night. It's not nice to make up stories. You were late, accept it and your punishment. There's no such thing as giant rats." She smiled then. "I'm actually surprised at you. I would've thought you could've come up with a better lie than that. You really thought we'd believe you? Take it as a fact?" She shook her head. "Why do kids always think their parents are so stupid?"

"No, Mom, I swear it's all true, I wasn't making it up." He told her that the story about wild dogs wasn't true either.

She frowned and looked her son in the eye. "Honey, that's crazy. And even it was true, how could you know this?" She looked at him with a quizzical expression.

Domenic was about to tell her everything that had happened last night, about the white vans, the SUVs, the men in black chasing him, all of it, but stopped himself just in time. If she didn't believe any of the other stuff he'd told her, why would she believe the rest? And if he tried to prove it, she would no doubt be so angry that he'd snuck out in the middle of the night that she would ground him until he was twenty-one. No, he needed to keep quiet. It wasn't worth the risk.

"I heard someone talking at school. That's all," he lied, hoping she wouldn't see through his falsehood.

She patted his arm. "Oh, honey, that wasn't true, people are scared, they make things up, especially kids. You know this. Now, I want you to take the school bus home today. No walking, all right?"

He nodded. "Sure, I got it, no walking."

"Good." She checked the clock radio on his nightstand. "Now, come on before you're late. I want your teeth brushed and face washed and down in five. Okay?"

"Okay, Mom, I hear ya."

She leaned over and kissed his forehead, and with a smile and his dirty laundry in her hands, she left the room.

He was still very tired, and it felt hard to move, like his muscles were trapped in cement. He wanted to sleep for a week, but after everything he'd just heard and talked about with his mother, he knew even if he was allowed to, he couldn't go back to sleep—not anymore.

With no choice in the matter, he slid out of bed and began to get dressed. He already knew he was going to skip brushing his teeth; he was too tired. But he would wet the bristles in case his mother checked, knowing a little Scope would do the job.

- 12 -

The school day was half over and Domenic was still on edge.

Sitting in math class, he kept expecting the men in black to barge into his classroom at any second and take him away. He was confident the men that had chased him the previous night didn't know who he was...but still.

Chad Morgan was sitting to Domenic's left and he could see his friend was agitated. Domenic's legs kept shaking like he had to use the bathroom and he continually checked the wall clock, as if wanting to make class end faster by using his willpower alone. Luckily, only a few more minutes were left, and Chad had no doubt Domenic would jump up and run out of the room screaming for some unknown reason.

The teacher, Mr. Flowers, was droning on about fractions. When he turned to write something on the chalkboard, Chad leaned over to Domenic and said, "Hey, what's eatin' you? You gotta date?"

"Huh?" Domenic asked, pulling his eyes away from the door.

"You're actin' awfully itchy today," Chad said. "What's wrong?"

"Mr. Morgan, do you have something to add to solve this problem?" Mr. Flowers asked as he gestured to the math problem on
the chalkboard. He sounded bored, he always did.

"No sir."

"Then I suggest you be silent and pay attention." Mr. Flowers
turned back to the chalkboard and continued to drone on.

"I'll tell you later," Domenic whispered. "Now shut up before
we both get detention."

Chad was about to say something else when Mr. Flowers
turned around again, glaring at Chad and Domenic. Chad
slumped in his chair and Domenic merely smiled, as if he had no
idea what was wrong.

Mr. Flowers sighed and weighed his options about what to do
with the two boys. Deciding he didn't feel like being a disciplinarian at the moment, he turned around and began working on the
problem again, but not before eyeing the two boys hard enough to
let them know they were on thin ice.

Domenic glared at Chad, who smiled slightly.

There were a few snickers from the other kids in class, a few
who had wanted to see the two boys get in trouble, but no one
said anything. Domenic glanced at the seat Emma would normally
occupy and his heart went out to her, knowing what had happened.

Then he heard a noise in the hallway and his heart jumped in
his chest and almost out of his throat!

It was them! The men in black were here!

A shadow came up to the door and Domenic was already half
out of his seat when he saw the janitor walk by, pushing his mop
bucket. After letting out a loud sigh of relief, Mr. Flowers turned
around and glared at him yet again. But Domenic barely noticed
the man, too relieved to see he was safe.

Mr. Flowers was about to open his mouth and chastise Domenic yet again, when the bell for the end of class finally rang. Students jumped to their feet and began talking immediately, filing out in twos and threes.

Mr. Flowers was going to pull Domenic aside before he left class, but the boy was nowhere in sight.

Domenic was already halfway down the hallway.

- 13 -

Study hall was Domenic's next class and Chad was with him as well. They never had the same teacher twice. It seemed whatever teacher was free that period would end up being the teacher.

As Domenic entered the classroom, he was pleased to see it was Mr. Allen, who was the psychology teacher. He liked Mr. Allen, who he considered to be one of the 'cool' teachers on staff. Mr. Allen didn't mind if the kids talked amongst themselves, as long as they were quiet and no one used a cell phone.

Everyone knew he really didn't mind even that, but the school had a strict policy of no cell phones in use during school hours — with the exception of at lunch if the students were outside in the schoolyard.

Mr. Allen looked up from the newspaper he was reading as he sat behind his desk and nodded politely to Domenic, then went right back to reading the sports scores. That was one of the things Domenic loved about Mr. Allen, the simple fact that he treated kids with respect, almost like equals.

Domenic picked a seat in the back of the room. He always tried to get a seat in the back, that way he could get away with whatever he wanted, whether it was playing games on his cell phone or talking to another kid in class. Unfortunately he didn't have his cell phone, having lost it when he was attacked by the rats. He planned on waiting for as long as he possibly could before telling his mother. He knew his father wouldn't be pleased at having to replace it.

Chad entered the class with a few other kids and quickly joined Domenic in the back. He dropped his backpack on the white tiles and plopped down in his seat like he was eighty years old with a bad back and arthritis.

"Man, what a day," he said with his head leaning way back. He slowly swiveled to face Domenic, who was grinning as he watched his friend's antics.

"Feeling your age, Chad?" he asked with a wide grin.

"Ha, ha, oh man, you're so funny. Hell, you should take that act on the road. I mean, it's just not fair that only humble me gets to experience your wit and charm. The whole world should get to see you." Chad was on a roll, something he was fond of doing. When this happened, Domenic would lean back and listen, sometimes nodding if the need arose.

"Keep it down, please," Mr. Allen said from the front of the room. His head never left the hidden recesses of the newspaper.

Chad sat up straighter while the rest of the room quieted down a little. Domenic knew in about five minutes the noise level would go up again, then Mr. Allen would ask again and the cycle would continue until the bell rang forty-three minutes later.

"So, Dom, you wanna tell me what was up in Math class?"

"What're you talking about, Chad?"

"Come on, really? You're really gonna play me like that? Dom, I know you, man. I mean, I *really* know you. We've been friends for years, since first grade. I saw you watching the door like you were expecting to be taken away at any second. So spill it, what did you do? Are you gonna get expelled? Detention? Suspended? What, come on, spill it already."

"I don't know what you're talking about."

"Dom, listen, you know me, too, and believe me when I tell you I'm not gonna let up till you spill it. So come on, what did you do?"

Domenic bit his lip, thinking about his next move. Of course he wanted to tell someone about the rats, but the question was if Chad would believe him. Hell, he'd been there last night, seen the giant rat and the men in black, but now that it was daylight and it was in the past, he had a hard time believing it had all been real.

"Okay, I'll tell you but you have to promise not to laugh and most of all, you need to keep it a secret," Domenic said in a low voice, almost a whisper but not quite.

"Sure, sure, whatever, just spill it."

Domenic did, telling Chad everything that had happened to him since he'd been attacked by the giant rats. He finished up with the chase by the men in black, then leaned back and looked at his friend, waiting to hear what Chad would say.

At first Chad said nothing, his face solemn as he took it all in. Then he nodded slowly and said, "I thought it was wild dogs that were attacking people. That's what the news said." He frowned. "But you're saying it's all a cover-up?"

"Hell yeah I'm saying it."

"But why would the authorities do that? It makes no sense."

Domenic slapped his forehead and the noise made Mr. Allen look up from his newspaper. Domenic smiled at the man and Mr. Allen nodded back, then went back to reading.

"They're doing it 'cause they don't want anyone to know about the rats, stupid," Domenic hissed in a low whisper. "That's the definition of a cover-up."

"Okay, fine, if what you're saying is true, then what are we supposed to do? I mean, those rats are eating kids. That's us!" He was whispering too but loudly. He lowered his voice but no one had noticed.

"I have a plan." Domenic said. "After school I'm going to the police station. I'm gonna spill the beans, tell it all. Once the police know what I know they can take care of this mess. They can deal with the guys in the suits."

Chad nodded in agreement. "That's a good idea. The cops should be able to sort this out. I think you need to ask for a detective. They're the ones who do the investigating and shit."

"Thanks for the tip, I'll do that."

- 14 -

Domenic picked the school bus that would take him into the center of town. He sat with a few kids he knew and the ride was pleasant, and it was far too short before he had to get off.

He was two blocks from the police station, and as he walked, he found himself slowing down considerably, as if he was trying to put off reaching his destination.

This was at the back of his mind and he didn't even realize he was doing it.

Ten minutes later he was standing before the police station. Three squad cars were parked diagonally in front of the building, and other than a man in a business suit walking up the stone steps, it was quiet.

Domenic turned around to look at the street; that looked ordinary, too.

His eyes went to the alley across the street and the shadows within and a shiver went down his spine at the thought of what might be lurking within there.

Swallowing the lump in his throat, he turned and jogged up the steps, reached for the door handle, opened it, and stepped inside the station.

- 15 -

The inside of the police station was set up a lot like old television shows and movies about cop shows.

There was a raised desk-like podium in the front of the room, but where at one time it would have been opened to the public, now it was built into a wall and bulletproof glass covered the upper portion.

A glass door was to the right of it, and if buzzed through, a person would enter the main part of the station, where desks, file cabinets, and in the far back a small break room and conference room was located.

The building was built in the early 1900s and had never had much of a facelift on the inside or out other than a paint job now and then, and the separation of the main floor by way of the wall and glass door.

The basement floor, where the cells were kept, was old and there were even a few spots where the floor was open and someone could look up into the next floor.

The boiler leaked, and was very likely the original one. The heat had cold and hot spots, and the air conditioning was a crapshoot at the best of times.

In the winter, anyone riding a desk would have their own space heater with them, but even then they had to be careful or they would blow a fuse. The city knew how bad the building was but there was no money in the coffers to fix it up.

The mayor was hoping for Federal aid and if it went through, there were plans to close the old station down and build a new one across town. So far, it was all talk.

Domenic knew none of this, and in truth, would have cared less about any of it.

As he stepped inside the small foyer, a man sitting at the high desk, hunched over with his arms crossed before him, said, "Can I help you, kid?" It was the desk sergeant.

Domenic could just see the officer's name tag. It was **MURPHY**.

"Uh, yeah, I uhm, I need to speak to a detective."

Murphy leaned over some more so he could get a good look at Domenic.

He saw a clean cut kid with blonde hair that needed a haircut, a little wiry, maybe could be on the track team in school. His jeans were a little baggy, but not hanging down on his ass like some of the kids Murphy would see on the streets. Domenic looked like a decent kid. "A detective, huh? What about?"

"It's about those attacks, I know what's really going on," Domenic said. He was so nervous he felt like he would fall down right there.

Murphy set his jaw and gave the kid another once over. Maybe he'd been wrong about his assessment. "Oh, and what's really goin' on?"

"That's what I need to tell a detective."

"Well, kid, before anyone talks to a detective, they have to go through me. I'm what you call a bullshit detector. I make sure you're not gonna waste the detective's time. So you gotta tell me a little of what you know before I'll let you talk to one of the gold shields. You got me?"

"I…yes, sir. I guess so. Okay, so here's what I know. It's not wild dogs attacking everyone, it's rats."

"Rats huh? What the hell are you talkin' about, kid?" He looked out the door to the street beyond, like he was searching for someone, perhaps more kids. "Is this some kind of a prank?"

Domenic shook his head vehemently. "No, sir, not at all." He then told his entire story, from being attacked in the alley all the way up to the chase by the men in black. When he was done, he had to admit he felt better. Keeping all that in had been harder on him than he'd known.

Officer Murphy's face never moved while he listened to Domenic, not so much as a flick of his nose. Only his eyes blinked, as he stared intently at the kid before him who was telling him that there were giant rats in the sewers and men in black were running around the city in the middle of the night.

"Listen, kid, do you understand it's against the law to file a false police report? Now, I don't know if this is a prank, or if one of your friends put you up to this on a dare or whatnot, but it isn't funny. People are dead, son. Don't you understand that?"

"Yes, sir, I do. That's why I need to talk to a detective. If this doesn't stop, more people—more *kids*—will be killed."

"Look, kid, I'm gonna give ya a break, all right? Just get out of here right now and don't let me see you here again. You're lucky you found me in a good mood."

The phone rang and he answered it, talked for a few seconds, then hung up. He scribbled something down on a notepad, and when he looked up, he was surprised to see Domenic still standing there.

"But you don't understand," Domenic pleaded. "Everything I said is the truth. You have to help me. No one is protecting the kids! We're not safe!" His voice rose in pitch as he began to get upset, frustrated that the desk sergeant wasn't listening to him. By the time he finished, he was all but yelling.

"That's it. Try and be nice and what do you get?" Murphy growled to himself loudly. He slid off his chair and began to walk around to the glass door. "You stay there, kid. I want your name and address. I'm calling your parents and they can come and get you. Maybe that'll knock some sense into you."

"Uh-oh," Domenic whispered, realizing this wasn't working out the way he'd planned. Murphy was at the glass door and was calling to another policeman. "Hey, Mac, buzz me out, will ya?"

Joe Macintyre, an officer with a pot belly from far too many donuts, walked over to the desk and pressed a button. There was a soft buzzing sound as the door was unlocked.

Murphy opened the door.

At first Domenic was frozen in place as Murphy walked over to the glass door, but he soon snapped out of it, understanding the officer wasn't his friend and in fact if he did what the man said, he would be in a world of trouble with his parents.

So he did the only thing he could. He turned and pushed through the outer door and began to run down the stairs to the sidewalk.

"Hey, kid, get back here, goddammit!" Murphy yelled, all out of patience. He charged through the door and onto the steps after Domenic.

But Murphy wasn't in the best of shape, and by the time he reached the bottom of the stairs, Domenic was halfway down the street and turning the corner, lost from sight.

Murphy stood before the police station, his hands on his hips as he huffed and puffed.

"Ah screw it, he's not worth it." He turned and slowly walked up the stairs, sweat stains already appearing under his arms. As he entered the police station, for the tenth time in as many weeks, he swore he was going to cut down on the fatty foods and hit the gym.

At the corner and hidden in a store alcove, Domenic peered back down the street. He imagined a dozen police officers running after him, waving guns and billy clubs. But as he stared at the street, all he saw were pedestrians walking, a few on cell phones and one mother with her child beside her.

The child was crying about something and the mother had an annoyed face plastered on her pale visage. Domenic wondered if the woman knew about the rats or even the made-up story of the wild dogs. If so, why would she take her child outside? Maybe she thought she was safe in the daytime with people all around her.

He watched the street for a full minute, and when no one came charging around the corner, he let out a heavy sigh, knowing he was safe. The desk sergeant had either lost him, gave up, or hadn't bothered in the first place to chase him.

He stepped out onto the sidewalk and began walking. He had a long walk home and didn't like being out like this—all alone, exposed.

Maybe the woman with the child was the lucky one, not knowing what was really going on, how deadly the situation truly was.

As he crossed the street and turned a corner, he paused as his eyes glanced at a sewer opening in the curb. He stopped walking and stared at the dark rectangular hole.

Was it his imagination or were there a pair of small yellow eyes peering back at him. He squinted to try and see better, but then a truck rolled by, the back end jouncing as the stiff shocks hit a bump, and when the truck was gone, so were the eyes. If he'd seen them at all.

He shook his head, thinking he must be going crazy. He was paranoid, that's all.

But as he walked on, he knew he wasn't paranoid when there truly were people or creatures out to get him. He'd already tried to tell his parents about the rats and they hadn't believed him.

He'd tried to tell the police but had received the same result. He had to face facts. No adult would believe him, and why should they? After all, in their eyes, he was just a stupid kid.

In fact, he could probably tell an adult their hair was on fire when it truly was and he would get a pat on the head and an accusing look that said he was lying.

Adults simply didn't believe children.

And if no one would believe him, and no one would listen, then the only way to deal with the rats was by himself. He remembered what Dr. Saunders had said about a nest.

That was it...the nest!

He needed to find it and destroy it before every kid in the damn city was killed by the rats.

His steps picked up as he walked with more determination now. He had a goal, he was taking back control. If no one would listen to him then to hell with them, he would deal with it himself. But he wasn't stupid, he knew he would need help.

Chad would assist him, he knew this, even if his friend didn't truly believe Domenic's story, he knew his friend had his back.

He knew Chad was the one person—the one kid—who would trust him without question.

But there was someone else who would believe him also. Not because they trusted him, but because they had seen the rats, too.

Practically running now, he passed street after street as he ran home, his eyes always searching the shadows for black creatures.

He knew exactly who he had to talk to. It was the only person in the world who would believe him without question.

- 16 -

Emma didn't stop crying until the day after her attack, after her Aunt Ruth had picked her up from the hospital and took her back home.

Emma's aunt lived only a block away from Emma's home, and as Emma lay in the guest room, and night fell on the second day, she could see—over the rooftops of the neighboring homes—the sky reflect the blue and red strobe lights of the police cars still around her house, as the authorities struggled to figure out what had happened and how Emma would have become an orphan overnight if not for her aunt taking her in.

Emma had been interviewed by the police to try and get to the bottom of what had happened. Only, no one believed Emma's story, as there were no rats to be found, only the bloody remains of her parents and her dog.

When she tried to make them believe her, they had a psychiatrist come in, a stern man who came to the decision that Emma was in shock.

But Emma knew what she'd seen. Giant rats had killed her family, had tried to kill her as well. Somehow, she would make them believe her, the only thing was; she didn't know how.

She stayed home from school for the next day, then, on the third day, she decided she wanted to go back.

Her aunt said she didn't have to, that it was too early, that after suffering such a loss she should remain at home, but Emma wanted to get out of the house, away from her aunt's concerned eyes, to feel like a normal person again, to stop pretending that she hadn't lost her entire family in one night.

Of course she was sad, but she also missed her friends and the normal routine that school would bring. In many ways, she needed to return to school desperately, so she could focus her mind on something else.

Reluctantly, after over an hour of discussion where Emma rationalized why she wanted to return to school, her aunt agreed, knowing how stubborn Emma could be when she'd made up her mind about something.

She was also amazed at how strong Emma was being. Yes, she cried, but she seemed to be able to bottle the grief and then only release it when she chose to.

What she didn't know was that Emma was not only filled with the loss of her family, but with anger and hate for the creatures that had done this to her.

All that rage was bottled within her, only she didn't know what to do with it. She wanted to make the rats pay, but she knew she was only a little girl. What could one child do against a horde of killer rats?

She hoped to find the answer in school.

- 17 -

The next day at 7:50 a.m., Emma was in the principal's office.

"Are you sure about this, Emma?" Principal Mathews asked. "This is highly irregular for someone who has suffered such a devastating loss to return to school so quickly."

"Yes, sir, I know that. My aunt said the same thing, but really I'm fine. I've been crying for almost two days straight...and to tell you the truth, I think I'm all cried out." She sighed. "I just want to get back to my studies and try and get on with things."

"But don't you need to grieve, dear? I mean, your parents and sister aren't even in the ground yet. When is the funeral? Tomorrow isn't it?"

She nodded. "Yes it is and that's why more than ever I need to be somewhere that's happy, where people don't look at me and think, 'There's the kid whose family was killed.' "

He leaned forward. "I highly doubt that will be the case, dear. By now, the entire school probably knows what happened. If you go to class today, you know some of the children will ask you questions. Now, I don't think they mean to be insensitive, it's just…the curiosity factor and all that. Are you able to handle that?"

"Yes, sir, I think I can." She stood up.

He leaned back in his chair. "All right then, though this goes against my better judgment, your aunt was specific on you coming back and there's nothing in the school charter I can use to stop you. But remember this, please. If for any reason it becomes too much for you, or if you just need to talk, come and see me, all right?"

"Yes sir, I will."

"Promise me, Emma."

"I promise, sir. Thank you, Mr. Mathews."

"Okay then, get going or you'll be late for first period."

As Emma left the principal's office, the first bell rang for class. Domenic was walking by the principal's office and he saw Emma step out into the hallway. She turned and began walking and he quickly jogged to catch up to her.

"Emma, wait up, I need to talk to you," he called as she slowed and turned to see who it was.

"Oh. Hi, Domenic."

"Uhm, hi, listen, I'm sorry about what happened to your family."

Emma's faced took on a mask of pain and she lowered her head and gazed down at her feet. But when she raised her head, the look was gone, wiped away. "Thanks, it's been a tough few days and I cry sometimes, but my aunt is there for me. I know I have to be strong. It's just…"

"It's just no one believes what really happened."

Students walked by, talking and laughing while going to class, as Emma and Domenic stood near the wall out of the way.

Emma's eyes went wide. "What do you mean?"

"It was rats, wasn't it, Emma? Big ones. I know 'cause they attacked me, too, but I got away."

And then the floodgates were open and Emma began to cry. She thought she was strong enough to return to school but she was wrong. As she sobbed openly, tears running down her cheeks, Domenic stood by her, biting his lip uncomfortably.

What was he supposed to do? Should he hug her, pat her back and tell her it would be all right? Her entire family was killed; of course it wasn't going to be all right.

After a full minute she regained some control and through sniffles said, "So you know it was rats?"

"Uh-huh." He saw the hallway was thinning and he wanted to talk to her so he gestured she should follow him. "We can't talk here, follow me."

She nodded and they began to walk down the hallway. Domenic soon spotted a janitor's closest and he quickly led her inside it with him in the lead. When the door was closed, he began to fill her in on everything that had happened to him. When he was finally done, she looked as if a giant weight had been lifted from her, now knowing she wasn't alone.

She wrapped her arms around him, hugging him tightly. "Oh, Domenic, those things killed my mom and dad, they killed my baby sister Jenny, and they killed my dog! And no one believes me! They think I'm crazy!"

"You're not crazy. But you're right. No one believes me either. I tried and they all think I'm making it up. We're kids, Emma. No adults will listen to us."

"So what do we do?" She was sniffling but in control. Having a confidant was the best thing ever for her.

"We have to find the nest and kill them ourselves."

"Just the two of us? That's crazy!" she exclaimed.

He shook his head, his blonde hair falling over his eyes. "No, not just us. Chad will help and I'll get a few more kids that'll believe me."

"No one else will believe you," she said.

"Yes they will, I'll make them."

"But…" she began but was halted when the door to the janitor's closet was thrown open and Principal Mathews was there, glaring angrily at them.

"I don't know what the meaning of this is, you two, but you both have detention today after school." He looked down at Emma and frowned. "I don't know if you're acting out or what, young lady, but this kind of behavior will not be tolerated. Now, the both of you, off to class before I make it a week of detention."

"Yes, sir," they both said quickly and were off, practically running down the corridor.

"I think he thought we were making out," Domenic said as they ran.

"In your dreams," she replied.

"Hey, that hurts," Domenic said defensively.

Principal Mathews watched them turn the corner, shaking his head in confusion.

They were much too young for that kind of activity and for the girl to be doing it after all that had happened to her seemed absolutely shocking.

As he turned and walked away, he knew then he would be getting Emma into counseling immediately. Obviously the girl had more problems than losing her family, if that were even possible.

- 18 -

Domenic and Emma weren't alone in detention. There were four other kids with them. The teacher was a taskmaster named Mr. Edwards who didn't allow any talking or cell phones. The only thing they were allowed to do was their homework, and if that was finished, then they had to sit quietly.

Detention was an hour long. A few times Domenic heard Emma sniffling and saw her shoulders shaking, her hair covering her face. She was doing a good job of holding it in but he could see she was crying. He wanted to console her but knew if he so much as risked saying something, Mr. Edwards would jump on him.

Still, he couldn't blame her too much for being sad. He tried to imagine how he would feel if his entire family was slaughtered and he was the only survivor.

He didn't think he would be as strong as Emma, but he hoped maybe he was wrong and if such a terrible tragedy happened, that he would pull from within himself a strength he didn't know existed.

He just hoped if they got into trouble when dealing with the rats, that she would be able to keep it together.

Time passed slowly, but eventually Mr. Edwards slapped his desk and said, "All right, people, your time is up, you may leave." As everyone began gathering their belongings and exiting the room, he followed up with, "And if you don't want to visit me again, follow the rules."

Domenic and Emma shuffled out of the room, walking side by side.

"You okay?" he asked. "I saw you were crying some."

She wiped her nose with her sleeve and nodded. "Yeah, I'm fine. Like I said, sometimes it sneaks up on me, you know, me missing them. Sometimes I still can't believe it really happened, like it was some sort of nightmare. I keep thinking any second now my mom's gonna call me on my cell and tell me to get home before it gets dark out."

Domenic had nothing to say in reply so he stayed quiet.

"I keep thinking I can just go home tonight, have dinner with my parents, maybe play with my sister for a bit. Then I'll go to bed and my dog will curl up at my feet." She sighed and a shudder ran down her body. "But I know those days are long gone."

"I'm so sorry, Emma, I really am," he said.

"Thanks. Sorry to be throwing all this at you, it's just…you're the first person I can tell the truth to and you believe me."

They had reached the schoolyard and were both surprised to see the late bus was long gone.

"Damn it," Domenic muttered. "The bus left without us."

"What do we do?" she asked.

"We have to walk home. What else? Come on, we can cut across the park and then through the west end."

"You mean where all those old warehouses are?"

"Sure do, I used to go down there with Chad and play sometimes. Most of the buildings are empty and you can just go inside and look around. It's pretty cool actually."

She seemed hesitant so Domenic said, "Look, it's almost dark, but if we walk fast we can be through there and at our houses in twenty minutes, tops."

"But the rats, you said…"

"I know what I said, but the odds we find any of them are a million to one, hell, even better than that. We'll be fine."

"Okay, I trust you."

He puffed out his chest and smiled. "And you should, I know what I'm doing."

- 19 -

Tyler Jackson paused to rest as he finished up working in his backyard. The tree trunk had been a bitch to remove but it was finally out of the ground. Tomorrow, he planned on getting his neighbor to help him roll it into the back of his pickup, where he would then take it to the city dump.

As he drank from a dented plastic water bottle, he gazed over at his son on the other side of the yard, playing in his sand box with his favorite trucks. Josh was six years old with dark brown hair, ears that stuck out more than they should, and a smile that lit up any room he was in.

Tyler had never wanted kids, but when his wife, Wendy, broke the news to him that she was pregnant almost seven years ago, he found the news to be the best thing to ever happen to him. Having a child had changed his life, and all for the best.

He wiped his sweat-covered brow with the back of his arm and gazed up at the sky. It was getting dark and he knew Wendy was getting supper ready. Pot-roast, his favorite.

Wendy hadn't been much of a cook when he first met her, but over the years she had learned to do everything from fry up a pork chop to bake a cake. The only problem he had was when she tried something new, something she'd never made before. He would always smile and chew happily as she watched him, but inside he was slowly dying.

Wendy wasn't very good at new recipes, unfortunately.

But her tried and true meals, such as pot-roast, were always a winner in his book.

His stomach growled and he licked his lips in expectation of tasting that first cut of meat. Then, with a new resolve to finish up for the night, he got to work again.

He was so focused on moving the tree stump a few more feet away from the hole that at first he didn't hear his son cry out.

With his own grunting and his heartbeat pulsing in his ears, it hadn't sunk into his work-fueled mind. But then Josh let out another yell and this one—clearly filled with fear—chilled Tyler to the bone.

With the setting sun casting shadows across the yard, Tyler couldn't see too well what was going on at the sandbox, but he could see that his son was surrounded by dark shapes that seemed to blend into the falling shadows.

As his mind processed this, the news reports he'd watched came flooding into his mind.

Wild dogs. They were here, in his yard, and about to attack his child!

Reaching down and picking up the shovel he'd been using to extract the stump, he ran for his son, the shovel high over his head to crush the first dog he reached.

"Josh! Oh Christ, hold on, son, I'm coming!" he yelled.

The instant he called out, every single head in the yard swiveled to look at him, human and creature alike. At the exact same moment, a ray of fading sunlight creased the yard, illuminating the sandbox clearly.

What Tyler saw chilled him even more than the thought of wild dogs.

For the shapes were now exposed for what they truly were.

Rats.

And giant ones at that, all with teeth bared.

"Get the fuck away from my son!" he screamed and swung the shovel down at a rat. The metal clanged off a head and the rat's skull was crushed instantly, dark brains staining the grass scarlet. But as Tyler concentrated on killing one rat, three more dashed to the side and came up on his left flank.

They sank their teeth into his ankles and calves, making him falter and trip. He landed heavily in the grass, his face becoming buried in the moist sod. As he pulled his arms under him to get up, two more rats darted at his face, while the ones that had bit him jumped onto his back and began to bite his neck.

He saw it happen, as if it was a movie, only this film had been put on slow motion so that every frame could be seen clearly, each segment studied. He saw the two rats dart in with teeth dripping saliva and sink them into his left eye, while another did the same to his right one.

His vision worked for a few seconds after the rats each buried into his eye sockets and tore out his eyes. As he screamed, his eyes were withdrawn, the optic nerves still attached and stretching. He saw it all, though his vision was now nothing but the inside of the two rats' mouths.

Then each rodent pulled back and the optic nerves snapped, forever sending Tyler into a world of darkness. The rodents scuttled away to the side, dropped the eyes, and charged back into the fight.

He shrieked in pain and pushed himself to a crawling position, his pain-filled mind still thinking of his son. With pink ooze dripping out of his empty ocular sockets, he began crawling as the rats nipped at his arms and legs, some clinging to his back. He batted at them, shouted at them, screamed for them to leave him alone, but it did no good.

He was less than a foot away from the sandbox when his luck ran out and they swarmed over him, covering him from head to toe.

The rats on his back sliced through his shirt, blood soaking into the material. Then they began to tear at the back of his neck while one burrowed into his body after tearing a hole in his side with its teeth.

One rats' teeth found Tyler's carotid and sliced into it, the blood shooting out four feet into the air before the elicited scream fell short. He tried to shake them off him but was too weak from blood loss, and seconds after he began to lose blood, he collapsed onto the grass, the blood seeping from his neck wound to soak the blades red.

Once Tyler was dead they left him, for he was an adult and the meat wasn't to their liking.

But the little one, ah, that was another story.

Josh was crying as the rats swarmed over his small body, and he even tried to bat them away feebly. But he was far too young to understand what was happening.

All he knew was that the black things were hurting him, and as he screamed and cried, these were the thoughts in his terrified head.

The screams didn't last long, and the child was quickly killed by getting his throat torn out. As Josh died, the rats began to dissect him, their razor sharp teeth slicing through flesh and bone as if it were paper. As each arm and leg was severed, a rat would pick it up with its mouth and gallop away. The torso was heavier and was dragged away by a rat moving backwards.

As the rats took the pieces of the child away, three others gathered up the rat with the crushed skull and began to drag it away, too.

In no time they were through the bushes and into the next yard, where they would then continue on to a nearby sewer opening.

It all happened within minutes, and when Wendy came running into the backyard upon hearing Tyler and Josh's screams, all she found was her dead husband and a sandbox soaked in blood.

Her child was gone forever, never to be seen again.

- 20 -

They were halfway home when the rats appeared.

Domenic and Emma didn't see them at first, the rats following them from behind, but when a half dozen popped out and blocked their path, they realized they were trapped.

Wanting to get home, Domenic had risked cutting through another alley, thinking that the odds of coming across more rats was a million to one.

If only he'd been older, he would have played the lottery that night for he was either the luckiest or unluckiest person on the planet...and so was Emma.

She had spotted the rats first and Domenic had found out half a second later as she screamed and grabbed his arm so tightly that there would be a dark bruise there the next day.

When she screamed, he didn't know what was wrong, but then his eyes spotted the shifting black rodents in the shadows and he felt his bowels shifting inside him, his legs going weak from fear.

He grabbed her and turned around to run the way they'd come only to see their retreat was blocked as well.

"What do we do?" she gasped, tears rolling down her face in thick rivulets. She was shaking uncontrollably. The trauma of what had happened only a few nights ago was hitting her full force and she could barely stand up as she stared at the black horrors before her.

"Just give me a second," he said, his mind racing.

"We don't have a second. Oh God, they're gonna kill me, too!" she yelled.

The rats began to encroach on them, and when he looked over his shoulder, he saw the ones behind were also moving closer. They were taking their time, as if they knew their prey was trapped and helpless.

He knew there was no more time to waste. He had to act now or they would be overrun and killed.

Though terrified, he also knew that the rats were flesh and bone and could be hurt and even killed. Acting fast, he moved to the left a few feet and picked up the lid to an old metal trashcan. It was dented and had bits of dried gunk stuck to both sides of it but it was a serviceable shield given the tenuous circumstances.

"Get behind me," he said quickly. "And do exactly what I do."

"What are you gonna do?" she cried, her sobs wracking her body.

"There's no time to explain, just move like I do and hold on tight."

She did what he said and he winced as her hands locked onto his arms in a vise-like grip.

Domenic's gaze went to the rats before him, and he studied each one for half a second before moving on to the next. He was trying to see if there was anything different about one over another.

Then he saw it, though it wasn't much. The rat on the far right was a little smaller than the others and looked like it had a small limp. It was hard to see in the falling darkness but it was all he had to go on.

If he was correct, then he'd picked out the weakest link.

"Okay, stay close!" he yelled and he began to run at the rats, the rodents screeching and hissing as he approached. At the same time, the ones in the rear began to run at the two children, their sharp claws clicking on the pavement.

At the last possible second before the rats in front of him and Emma reached them, Domenic shifted to the right and used the trashcan lid as a battering ram and plowed into the smaller rat at the same moment the rodent lunged for his throat.

He felt the impact of the rat on the lid and there was a dull clang as the rat bounced off the lid and fell to the ground. It rolled onto its back and then its side, and an instant later was on its feet once more.

But that fraction of a second when it was knocked away was all Domenic and Emma needed, and they burst through the hole in the rat's attack line and were free.

"Run, Emma, run!" Domenic screamed and began to pull her as he dashed down the alley and into the night. Though terrified, his voice spurred her on and her feet were light as a feather as she raced after him, one hand never letting go of his arm.

Behind them, more than a dozen giant rats gave chase.

- 21 -

"This way!" Domenic yelled. "Follow me!" He turned left out of the alley and ran as fast as he could, Emma almost being dragged behind him as she held onto his arm.

An alley. What had he been thinking? He remembered his words to her. *The odds of coming across more rats is a million to one.* In hindsight, how wrong he'd been.

Before him was the small warehouse district. Four square blocks of nothing but storage units for people with too much stuff, a large lot where an import car company stored their excess vehicles, and a few buildings that were now empty, thanks to the dwindling economy.

"Where are we going?" Emma yelled. She risked a glance over her shoulder to see a small blob of a shifting mass. The rats were running close together, in the darkness looking like one ebony entity. With her head facing the wrong way, she lost her balance and almost fell and only Domenic's quick reflexes saved them both. If they'd fallen, they would have been overrun in seconds, the rodents' razor sharp teeth slicing them to ribbons.

Domenic's eyes were flicking back and forth as he ran, searching for where they could escape to. The rats were closing the distance, and if he didn't find someplace for them to go soon, it wouldn't matter anyway. He hoped there would be a dumpster they could climb on, then perhaps climb up the side of a building like he'd done before, but nothing could be seen that was usable.

With no other choice, he picked a building at random and ran for it, praying by some miracle the door he reached would be unlocked.

It wasn't that farfetched actually. With many of the buildings abandoned when the businesses closed down, the structures were major hangouts for teenagers.

Most of the doors and windows had been jimmied open from the inside or outside and more than one section of a window was broken, despite the lead-lined glass and steel mesh interior.

He was moving so fast he actually bounced off the metal door when he reached it, Emma running into him and pushing him into the door yet again. He pushed off and turned the doorknob.

The door was locked!

"Come on, we'll try another one!" he yelled and took off down the side of the building. Emma was right behind him.

A second later they were at another door. He reached for the handle, saying a silent prayer it would be unlocked, and his heart sank when the doorknob didn't turn. This one was locked as well!

"Domenic, they're gonna get us!" Emma screamed.

He turned to see the rats only a few feet away. Seconds was all it would take before they were on the two kids. His eyes darted along the side of the building, desperately searching for something that would be his and Emma's salvation.

Then he spotted it. A window six feet off the ground, the bottom panel open.

"This way!" he yelled and took off running. He didn't wait to see if she was following, his eyes locked onto the open panel.

When he reached it, he quickly gauged how high it was and how they would get inside. It didn't take long.

He spun around to face Emma, who was running straight at him. "Here, I'll give you a lift! That window!" he screamed and braided his fingers together into a step as he gestured to the opening with his chin. As she ran at him, he lowered his hands and she came at him, timing it so her left foot landed in his braided fingers. He lifted as soon as he felt her foot and up she went. Emma found herself flying for a brief instant and her hands went up before her. She managed to catch the lip of the window and her body slapped the brick wall.

Domenic got beneath her and pushed up with his hands. She slid into the opening.

Emma fell inside, and no sooner did she land then she was rolling to her feet and dragging a crate back to the window so she could poke her head out and help Domenic up.

She was just in time to see the rats swarm over him.

He punched a rat away and kicked another, keeping them at bay for only moments. He used those seconds bravely.

"Emma, listen to me!" he grunted as he fought the rats. "The nest! You have to find the nest in the sewer! It's the only way to stop them! Tell Chad, he knows! Ah, get off me, you bastards!" He screamed in pain when sharp teeth sank into both his legs and more found his arms. He lost a finger when a rat clamped its mouth shut, the hot blood squirting into its mouth.

Domenic tried to fight but there were too many, and as he turned and tried to escape, three more jumped onto his back, forcing him to the ground.

"Domenic, no! Noooo!" Emma cried as she reached for him.

All she could see in the shadows were black bodies spinning and turning around in a circle, four-legged sharks with claws and long tails.

A brief ray of light bathed the area for a moment, and in that instant, Emma saw a bloody hand shoot up through the chaotic swirl of black fur. The hand was wide open, then it closed into a fist, and it retreated into the mass of shadows.

"Domenic, no, you can't die! You can't!" Emma cried, tears rolling down her cheeks. She could barely see, her vision blurry, thanks to the tears filling her eyes.

Sometime she could see Domenic's legs, and from where she was they looked like they were moving. Yes, they were moving! He was still alive!

Then something odd happened. The left leg went one way and the right leg went the other. They were spreading so far apart from one another that it seemed impossible. Then she saw the top of his head and his face appeared, and her heart leaped into her chest. He was alive. He was fighting them off!

But then the head ducked down and was moving away from the mass of bodies. She stared in horror when she realized the head wasn't attached to Domenic's body anymore, and that a rat was carrying it in its mouth!

She saw his legs moving away, following the side of the building, and it hit her hard and fast what was happening.

Domenic was being taken apart and the pieces carried away.

"Oh my God," she choked and threw up right there. Her vomit splattered on the ground and hit more than one rat, covering their black fur in bile and juices.

One rat looked up and hissed, and a second later more did the same.

Suddenly, though feeling a terrible loss for Domenic, she found out she was still in mortal danger.

Five rats peeled off from the main pack and tried to reach her, jumping up only to fall back down when gravity took hold.

A few chattered to themselves and two more began sniffing the wall, then one found the second door Domenic had tried to open, but had found locked.

As Emma watched, she saw the rats begin to scratch the bottom of the door, their sharp claws scraping off the paint, and in no time a small hole appeared. With the hole there, a rat began to chew at the metal, the thin veneer no match for the powerful incisors. A rat could chew through cement; a door with a metal facade was no match.

"Oh no," she whispered, the sniffles slowing, her heart pumping even faster than before.

As another three rats dragged off Domenic's remaining body parts, Emma ducked back inside the warehouse.

As she jumped off the crate, her eyes went to the metal door, and already spots of wan illumination could be seen at the bottom.

They would be inside in less than a minute.

Turning, she ran deeper into the building, her mind racing on what to do next.

As Emma ran for her life, the first rat pushed through the hole in the door, followed by another, and then more.

In less than a minute, every single rat remaining outside was inside the building.

Noses twitched as they tried to sense where their prey had gone to. It only took a moment for one of the rats to pick up the scent and take off running, a high-pitched squeak signaling the others to follow.

The hunt was on.

- 22 -

Emma's feet slapped against the concrete, echoing off the steel pipes and brick walls around her. She was scared, so scared she could barely breathe. She was soaked with sweat, tears streaming down her face, blending in with the perspiration droplets already there.

How could this be happening? It seemed so surreal, like something out of a horror movie.

Domenic was dead, and she'd seen it happen. She'd watched as his body was torn apart by giant rats. When she thought about it, she told herself it couldn't be real, but she'd seen it, she knew... She knew!

She could hear them behind her, searching, calling to one another in high-pitched squeaks.

She needed to escape, to find a place of safety, but there was nowhere to go. On each side of her, one foot diameter pipes lined the walls horizontally, and above, she could see steel catwalks far too high to be attainable.

There was no electricity, and any light solely filtered in through the dirty windows lining the outer walls.

She stumbled and almost fell and reached out to catch herself from falling. Her right hand reached out to stop her. Her palm touched one of the pipes, and no sooner did it land on the metal, then she pulled it back.

The pipe was hot. Her eyes caught the word **STEAM** etched on the pipe and then spotted a wisp of steam leaking from a valve on the top of it.

With this knowledge, she played her eyes over the other pipes and saw that more than half of them were steam pipes. A few had pressure gauges on them as well, though she had no time to read them and probably wouldn't understand what it meant even if she did.

With nowhere to go but deeper into the factory, she ran, soon lost in the maze of steel and concrete.

She stopped running and stood still at a junction, trying to get her bearings.

It was as she stood there, her breathing coming in deep gasps, that her peripheral vision caught something dart past her a few feet away. By the time she turned her head, the shadow was gone; she took a step in the opposite direction.

Another blur came to her right and her head swiveled quickly, her hair swaying around her face. Still, the blur was gone by the time she tried to look at it head on.

Tense, her reflexes on overdrive, she tried to filter out the hissing of the steam pipes and listen for any sounds beneath it. Another blur and this time she was ready. Spinning around, she spotted the thin tail of a large rat as it flew past the opening to her right.

A skittering sound came on her left and she spun to see another rat, only this one was standing there, glaring at her, its whiskers flicking, its front right paw wiping its muzzle as it cleaned off blood from its face.

She knew it was Domenic's blood.

More shadows behind the first rat appeared, lining up one at a time. The rats positioned themselves like bowling pins, then spread out more in the back of the line. To her left, and right, she saw more gathering as well.

She turned, preparing to run in the only direction left to her, but before she took so much as one step, she found her escape blocked by half a dozen rodents, all dark black, all with glowing eyes that filtered what light remained in the factory.

She was trapped!

She was surrounded with no possible chance of escape.

That was why they hadn't attacked; they knew she wasn't going anywhere. They could take their time, savor the kill, feed on the prey's fear.

One at a time, they began to walk towards her, mouths already opening in anticipation of the kill.

- 23 -

The rats were no more than six feet away when something dropped down from above and hit Emma on the right shoulder. At first she thought it was another rat, one that had somehow managed to climb into the maze of pipes to drop down from above.

But when she reached up with both hands to brush off the rodent, her hands hit a thick, hanging electrical cable instead. She didn't understand and only stared at it stupidly.

"What the hell are you doing?" a voice called from above. the face lost in the shadows. "Climb up before they get you!"

At first she did nothing, merely continued to stare at the cable, but then a rat nipped at her leg and she snapped out if it. Reaching up, she began to climb the cable.

Unfortunately, she didn't have the upper body strength to go very high and four feet off the floor, she stalled. A voice rang in her head, that of Coach Chambers, the gym teacher. He was telling her and the rest of the gym class the importance of staying in shape, and one way was to climb the braided rope with knots every foot in it.

Of course, everyone in class thought it was stupid, and only two girls out of the seventeen in class that day could even reach the top and half of the class could barely make it to the halfway point.

But now, as she hung by her hands, her fingers screaming that they would be letting go at any moment—and thus the betrayal would allow her to be killed by rats—the irony of Coach Chambers' talk wasn't lost on her.

She managed to look past her raised right arm to see the rats circling below her. A few were jumping up at her, their teeth nipping at her sneakers, but each time they couldn't find purchase and fell back to the hard cement floor.

"What are you waiting for?" The voice called down. "Climb up already!"

"I can't, my arms are too tired!" she gasped back, her arms now shaking from the strain.

She felt something tug her right sneaker and looked down to see a rat was hanging onto her. Its teeth were clamped on the rubber of her sneaker heel, its tail flicking back and forth. It may have managed to get a grip but it couldn't do anything else but hang there.

She tried to shake it off, but it was on too good and each time she tried to kick out, her hands threatened to give out. Frankly, she didn't know how she was managing to still hold on. Fear probably, and terror, the terror of knowing what would happen to her if she fell.

Her mind flashed back to Domenic being dismembered and a chill ran down her spine at the thought of that happening to her, too. The added weight of the hanging rat was making it worse and she struggled to hold on, knowing she was losing the fight.

One rat that was more acrobatic than the others jumped up and latched onto the cable, then began to pull itself up it. It made it as far as Emma's sneakers and then couldn't go further, thanks to her feet moving constantly and threatening to knock it off. It hissed and waited for a chance to scurry up some more and reach the young flesh waiting above.

Below Emma was a sea of rats, all circling and jumping to get her. The sight reminded her of sharks in a feeding frenzy, something she'd seen on the Discovery Channel on Shark Week.

Her fingers were about to give, there was nothing she could do about it. Praying to hold on for just one more second, she gritted her teeth as her fingers turned white and began to slip. She dropped an inch, then another.

Below, the rats went wild, sensing the end was near and soon they would be feeding on young meat.

But then, just before she let go, she found herself being raised a bit at a time. Looking up, she saw the figure was pulling on the cable, foot by foot, slowly bringing her up.

Though she was ready to let go at any moment, she gritted her teeth and willed her fingers to remain where they were…for just a little longer.

On her sneaker, the rat still hung by its teeth, the tail flicking back and forth. Its beady eyes were locked onto Emma and spittle slid from between its partially open mouth. Its added weight was becoming too much for her.

"Please hurry," Emma called out. "I can't hold on any longer!"

"A few more seconds," the figure huffed. "You're almost there."

Emma screamed when she felt something furry brush her arm. She craned her neck downward to see a rat practically staring at her. It was the one that had climbed up the cable. It had squeezed past her shifting body and was now ready to sink its teeth into her neck.

She shrieked one more time, her eyes wide in terror as the rat prepared to lunge for her throat.

Then a hand reached down and grabbed the rat behind its neck, the scruff of fur bunching up in the hand. As the rat hissed at this unforeseen attack, it let go of the cable and the hand yanked back, the rodent falling away.

It dropped to the floor below where its head connected first, imploding like a rotten melon, spraying blood and brains in all directions. Emma saw its head fracture and swallowed hard, knowing that could be her in a few seconds if she didn't hold on.

Though she had tried her best, she simply couldn't hold on any more, and as she let out a blood-curdling scream, her hands slipped and she felt herself falling.

But the same hand that had pulled the rat off her was now snapping down and wrapping around her right wrist. Emma was jolted to a stop.

"I got you!" the figure said and began to pull her up.

There was a metal railing with cross bars lining the walkway and Emma reached up and wrapped her arms around the lower bar. She used the crook in her arms to hold her, for her hands had no strength in them.

She felt the weight on her right sneaker and remembered there was a rat attached to it. She screamed again, the inside of her throat becoming raw from all her yelling.

"Hang on, I got it!" the figure said, and when Emma looked up, she saw her mysterious savior was a boy around her age. He was handsome, with dark brown hair, brown eyes and a strong frame. He was holding a three foot pipe an inch thick, and it was raised above his head.

To Emma, it looked like he was about to clobber her with it. She screamed again as the pipe came down, imagining the feeling of the pipe striking her skull, the dull clang she would hear inside her head. Then she would be falling, the rush of air past her ears, her tears drying before she hit the floor, her body broken beyond repair to then be fed upon by the rats.

The pipe flew by her head, so close she felt the wind of its passing. The rat on her sneaker shook when it was hit but its teeth held tight. The boy raised the pipe again, and with even more strength, struck it again.

Cursing softly, he raised the pipe once more, this time aiming for the rodent's skull. As the tip connected with its forehead. the rat let go. Its legs twitched spastically as it tumbled to the floor below.

The others moved away as it hit the cement floor hard, its body cracking open to become another red stain a second later, its shattered carcass spraying intestines and blood in a circular pattern. The other rats hissed and squeaked, their prey now unattainable. They went wild, seeing another of their kind slaughtered by the prey that should be dinner.

"Here, let's get you off that railing," the boy said and Emma was helped up and over the railing. She dropped heavily to the catwalk and lay on her back, stunned by her escape, horrified by everything she was experiencing.

She wanted to close her eyes, and when she opened them again, to find out she was in her bed, safe, and her family was still alive and it had all been a terrible nightmare.

But she knew this wasn't true; it was all real, every blood-soaked second of it.

"Are you all right? Did they bite you?" he asked.

At first she didn't respond, merely laid there with eyes squeezed closed, then slowly she came back to herself.

"Hey, can you hear me? I said..."

"I'm fine...I mean, no, I didn't get bit." *Fine*. That was the *last* thing she was right now. "Just give me a second, okay?"

"Sure, no problem. I'm Roger Gilford by the way."

"Emma," she said softly.

He nodded at this information. He leaned on the railing and looked down at the rats. They were swirling still, round and round, heads tilted up in hunger.

"You're safe up here," he said. "They can't get to us."

"Yes, but we can't get down either, not without them attacking us."

"Yeah, good point," he agreed.

"There's a ladder around the far side of the walkway, but last I checked, rats can't climb ladders," he said.

Emma sat up, rubbing her eyes with the backs of her hands. God she was tired. She couldn't ever remember feeling so tired, even upon the realization of the death of her family.

"Not that I'm complaining, but what are you doing in here?" she asked.

"Me? I always come here. I hang out here a lot actually. My parents fight a lot so I come to chill out with my PSP. No one knows about this place, even the bigger kids. They hang out in an old warehouse nearby but don't like it in here. I guess it's too hot for them but I kinda like it."

She did realize it was hotter than it should be considering the building was supposed to be closed. The steam pipes added to the temperature, she figured.

"It's a good thing I was here and heard you yelling. Then I saw the rats behind you and it was like, wow, that was something else." He looked down at the rodents. "They're so big, too. I've never seen them that big before." He knelt down beside her. "My grandpa was in Vietnam. He's told me stories about the rats there, how fat and big they got feeding on the corpses of all the dead."

"I don't want to hear about it, please," Emma said. "I've seen and heard about enough death to last me a lifetime."

He frowned. "Oh shit, I'm sorry. I wasn't thinking straight." He stood up and went back to the railing, looking down again. His hair fell across his face, hiding his eyes.

"It's okay. Thank you for helping me. I'd probably be dead right now if you didn't," she said.

He blushed. "Aww shucks, it wasn't much. Anyone would have done it."

She stood up slowly. A wave of dizziness overtook her but she closed her eyes and it passed. She stood next to Roger who was looking down at the rats.

"We need to get out of here," she said softly. "Do you have a cell phone? I don't."

He shrugged. "No, I don't have one either, my dad says they're not necessary." He gestured to the rats below with his chin. "There's no way down that those rats can't reach and corner us," he pointed out to her.

She sighed, her adrenalin dissipating, her heartbeat slowing. Though still in danger, for the present she was safe from harm.

Her eyes roamed along the walls of the building, to the ceiling, back to the walls, until finally stopping on Roger.

Two full minutes had passed, Roger not saying anything, wanting to give Emma her space.

When she looked at him, Roger returned her gaze, and now he saw something new in her eyes, something that wasn't there a few minutes ago when he'd first saved her. He saw hope.

"What?" he asked.

"I think I have an idea," she said. "Here's what we need to do."

- 24 -

Half an hour later, Emma was on the floor, running for her life through the twisting maze of steam pipes.

Behind her, the rats were closing in, each one battling for the front position to be the first one to take down the prey.

"Get ready!" Emma yelled as she ran closer to where Roger was supposed to be waiting for her. She tried not to think about what would happen if he wasn't in position, for it was too horrible to contemplate.

Rounding a corner, she began to sprint, the finish line in her mind only twenty feet away.

Then she was there, running past Roger, who was standing with a pipe in his hands, the weapon raised above his head.

"Now! Do it now!" she screamed and dashed past him, the rats only seconds behind her, if that.

There had been no trial run on her plan; there couldn't have been. The instant Emma had touched her feet to the cement floor, the rats were after her.

Roger lowered the steel pipe like he was chopping wood, his target a pressure valve on a particularly large steam pipe about a foot off the floor. The steel pipe struck the valve with a loud *clang*, the vibration riding up Roger's arm and into his head, causing his ears to ring.

Though he'd given it all he had, the valve didn't break, only bent downward.

The plan had failed—miserably.

"Oh shit," was all he said as he looked up to see a horde of rats coming right for him.

- 25 -

The plan was a simple one as far as plans go.

It had come to Emma out of the blue as she'd studied the steam pipes. She remembered how hot they were to the touch and figured if she and Roger could get the steam to explode out of one of the pipes while the rats were chasing her, they would be scalded to the point they would give up the chase. Then, in the confusion, she and Roger could run for the exit and escape.

Getting the rats to chase her had been the easy part.

Roger had gone to the far end of the catwalk and began taunting the rats. Meanwhile, Emma had gone to the ladder and climbed down.

She thought she was going to have to call out to the rodents to tell them she was on the floor, but no sooner did her left sneaker touch down, then one of the rats swiveled its head to look right at her. It hissed and took off after her, the rest following a moment later.

Then she was running…for her life…again!

She had to get far away so Roger could climb down. When it was clear, he was going to go to the corridor Emma had gone through before she'd found him. She would then circle around and come back, and when she dashed past Roger, he would knock the pressure valve off the steam pipe and dispose of the rats in scalding steam.

Well, that was how the plan was supposed to work.

But when she ran past Roger and saw him bring the steel pipe down in her peripheral vision, but then didn't hear the loud hiss of steam, she knew something hadn't worked out the way she'd wanted it to.

Coming to a stop, she spun around to see Roger standing there surprised, and beyond him, the rats were coming right for him. He was immobile, looking at the rats and the pipe in his hands like they were a figment of his imagination.

If she didn't do anything, he would be dead in less than a minute, she knew this instantly. And she knew she couldn't let that happen…not after what had happened to Domenic.

Taking off at a run back to Roger, her breath sliding out of her mouth in heavy gasps, she got to him three seconds before the lead rat reached him.

She ripped the steel pipe from his hands and pushed him out of the way, just as the lead rat jumped at her. It had planned on getting Roger but she would be fine as well.

She raised the pipe over her head and brought it down on the bent valve, the blow enough to break it off. The steel pipe in her hands kept going downward until it struck the floor, making her drop it as the vibration filled her body.

And then she could see nothing as steam erupted into the corridor, a massive cloud of heat-condensed air that blocked all sight.

Though she couldn't see what happened next, she could hear it.

The rat that was in midair was caught by the steam and it twisted in the air and bounced off Emma's chest, shoving her back a foot and out of the worst of the spray. When it landed, it was in no condition to continue the chase.

Its eyes had boiled in their sockets, half its face now scalded. Its black fur was singed on the right side where it had been hit by steam and now all it could do was lay on the floor, blinded and in pain.

The others behind the first rat had been moving too fast to stop and had charged directly into the path of the erupting steam. They were cooked on the spot, their insides boiled as the tremendous heat caused bodies to rupture as gases expanded.

The rats behind the first wave weren't hurt severely but they were halted in their tracks. They milled about the corridor, not wanting to get too close to the scalding steam.

The sound of their brethren screeching as they were boiled alive was enough to break even their driving need for the hunt.

Emma was stunned by it all and was still standing at the edge of the steam cloud. When she felt a hand on her arm, she screamed, but then Roger's face was an inch from hers so she could see it was him. She calmed slightly.

"Come on, we have to go!" was all he said as he pulled her along after him.

She followed, still too stunned to think clearly. The two ran, leaving the screeching and hissing rats behind.

When they were well clear of the steam, the air temperature dropped dramatically and it felt wonderful on their sweaty bodies.

Roger led the way to another exit and they both slipped through easily, Roger slamming and blocking the door behind them.

As they left the factory behind, Roger let out a laugh at being free and said, "Wow, Emma, that was so awesome how you took that pipe from me and broke that valve off. I don't want to think about what might have happened if you didn't."

She shrugged. "I just didn't understand why you only tried it one time."

"I guess I froze. Sorry."

"It's okay. Hell, if you hadn't saved me in the first place I couldn't have saved you in the second. So I guess we're even "

He nodded. "Works for me. We're even."

When they were a street over from Emma's aunt's house, she stopped and told Roger about Domenic and what had happened. It was the first time she'd had a second to think since it had occurred.

Roger listened to it all, sometimes asking a question, then listening some more. By the time she was through, she was crying again.

Roger reached out and pulled her close, hugging her. Though normally she would never have let a boy do that to her—

especially one she'd just met—this time she didn't mind and in fact welcomed it. She sobbed on his shoulder and he brushed her hair and told her it would be all right. She knew it wouldn't but she appreciated the sentiment.

When her sobs slowed, she pulled back from his embrace. In the moonlight, she looked into his eyes and saw how truly handsome he was. Without thinking about it, she leaned forward and kissed him on the lips.

His eyes went wide but he said nothing.

Emma looked down at her sneakers, feeling embarrassed. "I'm sorry, I shouldn't have done that. I hardly know you."

"No, I mean, it's fine, really. I liked it."

"I feel so silly now," she said and blushed.

"I'm telling the truth, it's fine. Actually, I kinda liked it. Listen, when all this shit is done, you know, and over. Maybe we could go the movies or something?"

Her next words were going to be, "My dad says I'm too young to date." But then she realized her father was dead, and so were her mother and sister. She began to cry, the grief hitting her from out of left field.

The hospital psychiatrist had told her grief came at off times and that she had to accept this and in time it would pass.

"Oh gees, oh wow, I'm so sorry," Roger said. "I didn't mean anything by it. Forget I said anything, really."

She sniffled and began to laugh and he looked at her like she was crazy.

"No, Roger, it's not you, really. I'm not crying because you asked me out. I'll be okay in a bit."

She explained about her parents and sister, then finished with Domenic's last words to her, how she needed to find the nest in the sewer or else it would never stop.

"I'm with you," Roger said. "Just tell me where and when."

"Tomorrow night," she said. "I'll call you tomorrow after school and give you the details. But before I can lock it down, I need to see one more person."

"Sure, Emma, whatever you need. I'm here for you." He quickly gave her his phone number after finding a pen in his back pocket. Emma wrote it down on her palm, not having any paper.

"Listen, I gotta go, my aunt's probably worried sick. And thank you again…for everything." She leaned forward and kissed his cheek, then ran off into the night.

Roger watched her recede into the shadows before turning and walking away. He touched his cheek, still feeling her lips there. He knew right then he would follow Emma into the depths of Hell if that was what it took to get another kiss from her.

- 26 -

Before Emma went to her aunt's house, she made a detour and headed to Chad's house to tell him what had happened tonight.

With trepidation, she ascended the four stone steps that led to Chad's front porch, and with a shaking finger, pressed the door-bell.

It opened before she was going to press it again and Emma found herself looking up into the face of Chad's mother.

"Can I help you, dear?" Chad's mother asked. She took in the state of the girl before her: her clothes dirty, hair disheveled, face covered in dirt and grime. What had this girl been doing this night? she wondered.

"I need to speak to Chad; it's important," Emma said.

Chad's mother frowned deeply. "Important? What's this about? I don't recognize you. Are you one of Chad's friends?"

"Yes, ma'am. Chad knows me from school. Look, it's really important that I talk to him right now."

Her frown never wavered. "Well, it is kind of late. And are you out all alone? Surely your mother's heard about the roving packs of wild dogs. It's not safe out alone."

The mention of her mother was like a dagger to Emma heart, but she remained stoic. If she broke down crying now, she'd never get to talk to Chad. And for some reason even she didn't understand, she needed to tell him now, not in school tomorrow where teachers would be watching and other kids would be listening. No, this had to happen tonight.

"Who is it, Mom?" It was Chad's voice. He was deeper into the house but had become curious who his mother was talking to.

With her frown so deep it was threatening to slide right off her face, Chad's mother turned slightly and said, "You have a visitor, Chad. It's someone from school. She says you know her."

Chad appeared at the door a second later. "Emma? What are you doing here?" he asked.

"I need to talk to you, Chad." She glanced at his mother. "In private. It's about Domenic."

"Dom? What about him?"

Emma stared at him, her eyes repeating what she'd just said.

Chad looked up at his mother. "Can I go out on the porch with Emma and see what she wants?"

His mother didn't look pleased but decided it would be easier to let her son speak to Emma so the girl would leave. "Fine, but stay on the porch, and if you see anything dangerous, get inside immediately. Is that clear?"

"Okay, Mom, I hear ya." He took a step out onto the porch.

"I mean it, Chad. Don't leave this porch, or else." His mother turned and walked away. "And leave the door open, too. I want to hear you if you need me."

"Fine," Chad said, dragging the word out. He joined Emma, who turned and sat down on the edge of the porch so her feet were on the top step, and her butt was on the main landing.

Chad dropped down next to her. "So what's this about? I never talk to you in school and now here you are at my house. And why are you so dirty?"

She didn't know how to say it gently so she just came right out with it. "Domenic's dead. The rats got him."

"What?" Chad didn't understand.

"It happened after school today," she began. "We were walking home and cut through where the old warehouses are and..." She told him everything, holding nothing back. By the time she was finished she was crying again, the tears making grooves in the dirt covering her face. Chad never asked any questions, just listened silently. But by the time she was done, he was crying, too, though he was more stoic, and other than wet eyes, remained strong.

"So that's why he isn't home yet," he said. "I've been calling every hour and his mom says he's not home. She's pretty worried, too." He wiped his wet face with the back of his shirtsleeve.

"They'll never find him. Maybe his bones," she said. "But for now his parents will just think he's missing. You can't say anything, you know that, right?"

"Of course I know that," he said angrily. "I'm not an idiot. Domenic tried to get people to listen about the rats and no one would. No one listens to us 'cause we're kids, it sucks, and now Dom's dead because of it."

109

"Yes, and that's why we need to deal with this on our own." She told him about Domenic's last words, about finding the nest and stopping the rats once and for all.

"And we won't be alone. Roger will help us, too," she said.

Chad now knew about Roger from the story she'd told him. His insides were torn up in knots and sadness was threatening to overwhelm him at the thought of his best friend being dead. It seemed impossible, but looking at Emma, seeing into her eyes, Chad knew she was telling the truth. Domenic was dead, the rats had gotten another victim.

Pushing the grief down deep, he set his jaw and said, "So when do we do this thing?"

"Tomorrow night, after our parents have gone to sleep, we'll all sneak out of our houses and meet up at my house. The police are gone now and other than police tape around the yard, it's empty."

"Yeah, uhm, about all that..." Chad began, wanting to give his condolences to Emma about her family.

"Don't, please," she stopped him. "I mean, thanks but don't say it. I just can't hear another person tell me how sorry they are. Just help me kill those damn things and we're good. I want them dead for all they've done to me."

"And Domenic."

"Yes, him too." She sighed. Though she felt terrible she also felt something else. She felt in control. She wasn't going to just be a victim. She was going to fight back. "But remember, you have to stay strong and act like everything's fine. Domenic's only missing and no one knows where he is."

"I can't promise anything but I'll try," he said, feeling tears welling up again.

Emma gave it some thought and then had an idea. "Okay, if you have to cry, then tell your parents it's about me and that I came here to talk to you because of what happened to my family."

He nodded. "Okay, that'll work. And I really am sorry."

"Thank you," she said softly.

"After school tomorrow, see what you can find in your house to bring as a weapon."

"Like what?"

She shrugged. "I don't know. A baseball bat, a knife, something to fight off the rats with."

"And then what?"

"I don't know. I'll try to come up with something tonight. Just trust me on this."

He didn't look very confident in her ability to lead. "All right, but I'll tell you this for the sake of being honest. I feel terrible about what happened to Domenic, but I also know I don't want to join him, either."

"I couldn't agree with you more," she said before leaving.

- 27 -

Under the street, the sewer tunnel was dark, only the barest hint of light penetrating through the small holes in the manhole cover.

Only the sound of dripping water broke the silence. Then a hooked tool was slid into one of the holes in the manhole cover and grunting could be heard as it was dragged away.

Light spilled into the tunnel, still faint, but compared to before it was like a spotlight had been turned on. Feet appeared in the opening and then legs. Finally, an entire body appeared, followed by two more.

With Emma in the lead of Roger and Chad, she dropped down to the floor of the tunnel. There was an inch of water at the bottom, soggy leaves and old debris.

It smelled wet, reminding Emma of when her mother had worn a fur coat one night in the rain. She had put the coat back into the closet wet and the next day the same dank, musty odor she smelled now had permeated the closet...only much, much worse.

The water moved with a lazy current, and as she watched, the carcass of a small field mouse floated by. It banged off her sneaker to spin deeper into the middle of the current, then continued onward. She ignored it.

Emma looked up at the round hole and the night sky through the opening. "Hey guys, you need to pull that back on or else someone might find it."

"Aw, it doesn't matter," Chad said. "Besides, that damn thing is heavy as hell."

She glared at Chad and he held her gaze for a moment, then a second later he looked down, breaking eye contact. "Fine," he said, dragging the word out the way he had with his mother the previous night. "Hey, Roger, give me a hand, will ya?"

Roger nodded and the two climbed up so they were side by side at the top of the steel ladder embedded to the wall. With more grunts and groans and scrapes of metal on cement, they finally managed to get the manhole cover seated again.

"Watch your fingers!" she called up as the cover clanged like a giant puzzle piece back into its home.

"No shit," Chad said and began to climb down. Roger followed after him.

Their feet splashed in the water when they each jumped from the second to the last rung.

Emma stood before them, a flashlight in her hand. She let the light play over her two companions, her eyes catching the equipment and weapons each carried.

Roger was wearing a dark coat with pockets stuffed with cherry bombs. He had on jeans with holes in the knees. His sneakers were once white but were now so covered in grime and muck from inside the sewer that the color was impossible to see.

Chad wore a light windbreaker and carried a backpack, where he'd stuffed the items he thought he could use as a weapon. He also had his gear from hockey with him: a mask and body padding, the latter worn under his clothes.

Roger carried a plastic bucket full of balloons filled with gasoline taken from the five gallon plastic tank his father used for their lawnmower. It had been pointed out to him by Chad when he'd arrived at their meeting place that the gasoline would probably eat through the rubber of the balloons.

Roger had agreed with this assessment, but believed it would happen at such a slow rate that he would either have used them already or would be dead — killed by the rats — before it happened. And if he was dead, he wouldn't need them anyway.

Both boys were carrying baseball bats. Chad's was aluminum and Roger's was wooden. They also each carried a flashlight, a must if going spelunking in the sewers of the town.

Emma carried a duffle bag as well. Hers was filled with items raided from her aunt's garage. Hedge clippers, a blowtorch and a BBQ lighter were the things she found that she hoped would be of use. She also carried a butcher's knife taken from the kitchen. She wore jeans and a light jacket, and the same sneakers she always wore, though now they were coated with slime as well thanks to the water and sludge in the sewer.

She had been the first to arrive at the rendezvous in front of her old house. It had been a few minutes before two in the morning, the time they had agreed to meet up.

She'd stood there, feeling queasy, as she stared at her darkened home. The yellow police tape was still there, and as it fluttered in the gentle breeze, Emma wanted to scream that it wasn't fair, that she was all alone now. Yes, she had her aunt, but it wasn't the same. It never would be.

She had been so relieved when the boys arrived a few minutes later and she had an excuse to look away from her empty home and focus on the here and now. It was time for vengeance, and though some might say it wasn't enough to fill that deep hole of loss inside her, she knew if that was all she could hope for, it would have to be enough.

"So which way do we go?" Roger asked, breaking the silence that had fallen over them. He was looking at Emma when he said it.

She shrugged. "That's a good question. They could be any-where."

"Then we better get moving, there's miles to cover down here," Chad said as he slid his hockey mask on. "I'll take point. I have protection in case we get attacked."

Emma took up the middle and Roger was last.

"But what if they come at us from behind?" Roger asked.

"I guess you'll have to cover your ass...literally," Chad quipped.

"Ha, ha, man, you're so funny. You're quite the comedian," Roger replied back sarcastically.

"Will you two knock it off," Emma said, all seriousness in her voice and face.

"Sorry, Emma, just tryin' to lighten the mood a bit," Chad said.

"Yeah, sorry," Roger added. "I know how important this is to you."

Now she felt bad for snapping at them. After all, they were both down here in the sewer helping her, basically risking their lives for her. And for what? Because she asked them? Because Chad felt a loyalty to avenge Domenic? Then why was Roger down here?

If only she could see the way he was watching her butt as they made their way through the sewer, she would have known right then why Roger wanted to help. He'd fallen for her—hard.

"No, guys, I'm sorry for snapping at you. I guess I'm nervous...and scared."

"No problem, we all are," Roger said.

"Not me, I'm not scared," Chad said from the front. His flashlight beam moved back and forth as he made his way forward, pushing back the darkness a few feet at a time.

"Oh, man, you're so full of shit," Roger said.

Chad stopped walking and turned around, sliding up his mask. His face was illuminated by Emma's flashlight. "I'm not scared. I'm not afraid of a few rats. We can deal with them easy."

Roger chuckled. "That's 'cause you haven't seen them yet. Emma told you, they're not normal size, they're fucking huge...and mean. They'll tear your balls off before you know what hit you."

Chad swung his aluminum bat from side to side, though there wasn't much room for movement in the tunnel. "We'll see about that. I'll take them down quick and fast, you'll see."

"Will you two please stop, there's a lot of ground to cover and we only have till it gets light out," Emma said, butting in and trying to stop the macho posturing.

Roger looked down and Chad merely smiled, as if he'd won the argument. He pulled his mask down and began walking forward, his sneakers splashing in the water.

Every now and then, a whiff of something foul-smelling came to their noses. Emma tried not to think what it might be, but knew what the sewers were for, so she figured they were stepping in human waste.

They walked for more than an hour and were soon very lost. The sewer tunnels were a maze, each tunnel turning and bending more than the last one. Sometimes they had to duck down and practically crawl, and just when they would become scared it would never get bigger, it would reach a junction and open up.

Still, they found nothing.

A little more than four hours later, with all three of them tired and leaning against a tunnel wall, they rested and argued about how it was time to give up, that the odds of finding the rat nest was impossible.

Emma wanted to keep going but Chad wanted to leave. Roger was on Emma's side, though he was tired and was trying to convince her to maybe give up for the day and come back the next night and continue searching.

It was highly possible they could end up searching for days and never find a single rat, but the irony of the situation was that the rodents had found the children within fifteen minutes of them going into the rats' underground world.

There were five rats—scouts actually—and when they found the children, they were far from their nest and so had simply followed the kids, not wanting to attack for lack of numbers upon finding the prey in their habitat. One rat had been sent back to the nest a mile away to retrieve reinforcements, the other four staying on the prey's tail.

But the four remaining rats were hungry, and though they wanted to wait for more of their brethren, they also wanted to feed.

If the children had been above ground, no doubt the four rats would have waited for more of their kind before attacking, but they were feeling overconfident in their home turf, and with each passing second were growing braver and bolder.

- 28 -

"But I don't want to leave," Emma said for the fifth time. "We just have to keep looking. We'll find them."

"No we won't," Chad argued. "Listen, Emma, we've been down here for hours and so far all we've come across is some old toys, a few dead mice, and stuff I don't want to think about."

"He's talking about shit," Roger added with a grin.

Chad frowned and looked at Roger, his flashlight beam spearing Roger's face. "Yes, Roger, I'm talking about shit. We've been walking in it for hours and it's disgusting. My feet are soaked and my back hurts every time we have to duck-walk through another passage. I'm tired, I want to go home. This was a stupid idea, anyway. We're a bunch of kids for Christ's sake! We need to tell the cops and let them handle it."

Emma pushed off from the wall she was leaning on. "Don't you think that's what Domenic did? He did and no one listened to him. If they had, he'd probably be alive right now. Look, you do what you want, but I'm not giving up. Today's Saturday so there's no school. My aunt won't even think to check on me till ten in the morning easy." She had tears in her eyes and her arms were shaking as the anger inside her at Domenic's death began to rise once more. She wanted to lash out at someone, anyone, and Chad was making it easy for her to do just that.

But before she could begin to berate him, the four rats came rushing out of the darkness and jumped on Chad.

Only his hockey gear saved him from multiple lacerations from sharp claws. The weight of the rats was enough to knock him off his feet, and he cried out as he fell. When he hit the tunnel floor, his mask snapped back over his face. And just in time.

At the same time the hockey mask fell back down, one of the rats was darting in to take one of Chad's eyes with its teeth. Chad heard sharp teeth click on the hard plastic and saw the mouth agape directly over his right eye.

He was so taken by surprise that all he could do was curl into a ball and try to keep the rats from biting him somewhere vulnerable.

In the back of his mind, he also wondered what the hell Emma and Roger were doing while he was being mauled!

Emma was also taken by surprise. One second she was about to lay into Chad, and the next he was on the ground fighting off what looked like a half dozen rats.

Only when Roger shifted his flashlight to expose Chad did she see there were only four rodents, though that was still plenty in her opinion.

She stared in shock, too afraid to move, everything that had happened to her rushing back and filling her mind with dread, the terror freezing her limbs to the point of immobility.

Emma's flashlight fell from limp fingers to land in the water, the beam aimed right at Chad's flailing body.

Roger went into action almost as soon as he realized what was happening. Seeing Emma was safe and that no rats were near her, he shoved his flashlight into his pocket and picked up his wooden baseball bat from where it was leaning against the wall next to the bucket of gas-filled balloons.

"Get away from him, you little fucks!" he screamed and darted at the first rat, the bat raised over his head. They were in a section of the sewer with a high ceiling, though the bat still scraped the ceiling as Roger brought it over and down.

The tip connected with a rat, striking the rodent in the center of its back. It squealed in protest and twisted its head, as if to bite the offending weapon. Roger swung the bat to the side and whacked the rat in the side of its head, stunning it. The rodent rolled off Chad and splashed into the churned-up water as it regained its footing.

Roger kept swinging, striking each rat a heavy blow until they had all been removed from Chad, who jumped up the second there was no weight on him and holding him down. As he got to his feet, he reached out and grabbed his aluminum baseball bat.

"Fuckers jumped me," Chad hissed. "Thank God I wore this gear."

"No shit," Roger said. He looked at Emma. "You okay?" She didn't say a word, only stared at the rats. "Emma, snap out of it!" he snarled.

"Huh? What?" Emma said and slowly came back to reality. Her eyes refocused and she nodded. "I'm okay, I don't know what happened." She would have said more but a rat jumped at her. She raised her hands before her to ward it off, but Roger was there for her. Before it could reach her, in midair it was knocked away to bounce off the tunnel wall and land motionless, for the time being stunned. Its left rear leg was shattered and useless.

"Get behind us," Roger said as he raised the bat to ward off the next attack.

Emma did as she was told and got behind Chad and Roger, who waved their bats before them like swords. The three remaining rats were up again after taking a beating from Roger and were now prepared to continue the attack.

Only Roger had other ideas. "Come on, Chad, let's kill these fuckers!" he screamed and charged at the rats. Chad was right behind him.

Now it was the rats turn to be stunned as their prey came at them, yelling and screaming, not afraid in the slightest. One of the rats tried to attack but was quickly beaten into a bloody pulp, its blood seeping into the water to be lost in the swirling dark water. The other two were killed moments later, both with cracked skulls.

Chad had gone berserk and continually beat the rat he'd just killed, each smash of the bat pulverizing the carcass a little more.

Blood sprayed everywhere, on the walls, on Roger and Chad, and on the ceiling as the swinging bat sent castoff in all directions.

Roger let Chad go at it for almost a full minute and then grabbed the bat on its downward swing. "Enough, man, it's dead, it's fucking dead already!"

Chad still tried to raise the bat but Roger was larger and stronger than him and he held it firmly. Through the hockey mask, Chad's eyes slowly calmed and he lowered the bat for good. Roger nodded and stepped away to join Emma. She was huddled against the wall with her arms wrapped tightly around her.

She held the butcher's knife in her right hand and her flashlight in her left, but whether she could have used the knife if attacked was anyone's guess.

Roger watched her, wondering if she would be okay. She had been fearless the previous night in the factory but as he got to know her more, he saw there were times when she closed up to the point of being a danger to herself. If he'd been older, he might have recognized the symptoms of Post Traumatic Stress, but as it was, he just knew that sometimes she would flake out at the worst possible time.

She had a few drops of blood spray on her face and he reached out and wiped them off with his thumb, then wiped his thumb on his shirt to clean it.

"You all right?" Roger asked her.

"I'm fine, don't worry about me," she said and pushed past him to join Chad. She touched Chad's arm and he nodded to her, silently telling her he was okay.

Before any of them could say more, the first stunned rat that Roger had hit rose up on three legs, the fourth ruined to the point of uselessness. Emma heard the movement first and spun around, aiming the flashlight beam as if it was a weapon.

In the beam, the rat's eyes shone bright and it hissed and squealed. It looked as if it was going to attack, but at the last second, it turned and fled down the tunnel. It hobbled, barely moving faster than a light jog for a human.

Emma saw it flee and was immediately galvanized into action. "Follow it! It should take us right to the nest!" Then she was off, her feet splashing water in all directions as she ran heedless into the darkness.

"Emma, wait for us!" Chad called and began to run after her.

Roger, not wanting to be left behind, ran to the bucket of gas balloons, scooped it up by the handle, and took off running. His flashlight was in his left hand while he held the bucket by his wrist. The other hand carried the wooden bat, which was now covered in blood, black fur and bits of brain matter. He could feel the cherry bombs in his pockets jiggling as he ran.

In seconds, all three were lost in the darkness, only the distant glow of their flashlights remaining.

"Hurry up, we're gonna lose it!" Emma yelled as she raced after the wounded rat. It was up ahead, just at the edge of her flashlight beam.

If it hadn't been for the broken leg, she never would have been able to keep up but as it was, she was always able to keep it in sight.

"No we're not," Roger said. "Did you see that back leg? It was totally broken."

"Still," she said. "He's moving pretty fast."

And so the chase was on, the rat hopping through tunnel after tunnel.

Fifteen minutes later, it came to an intersection with a large square junction with four tunnels leading off in the four directions of the compass. It dove into the smallest one, about three feet in diameter, and was soon lost from sight.

Emma was about to follow it when Chad grabbed her jacket and stopped her. "Wait a second, Emma, we don't know what's in there or even if it's a dead end." He was breathing heavily, out of breath from the constant running.

They all were. Each of them was flushed with sweat and sucked in air now that they had stopped moving.

She turned to face him. "How can it be a dead end?"

Chad didn't have an answer. "I don't know, I'm just saying."

"He's scared, Emma, that's all. Come on, I'll go with you," Roger said.

"I'm not scared. I just think we should be careful, that's all. We don't know what's in there, it could be dangerous," Chad replied.

Emma stomped her foot impatiently. "We're wasting time; it's getting away!" She looked at Roger in the glow of her flashlight beam. "You'll come with me?"

"Hell yes," Roger smiled.

"Then it's settled." She spun around, tossed her duffle bag in before her, and crawled into the hole, sliding her body inside inch by inch.

"I hope you're gonna follow me, Chad, I could use the backup." Without waiting for a reply, Roger placed the bucket of gasoline balloons before him and then the baseball bat and crawled in behind her. Pushing the items before him, he began to follow.

Chad watched Roger's feet recede from view. He tapped his foot nervously and tried to decide what to do. He'd been brave enough at the beginning, sure, but after seeing the rats and how big they really were, well, he wasn't so gung-ho about this little adventure anymore.

But, after seeing and fighting the rats, he knew it was all true. Domenic was really dead, there was no doubt. Though he hadn't admitted it before, he'd kept a small amount of doubt in his heart after hearing Emma's story.

But she was so believable, even if the tale was farfetched, and when he'd called Domenic's house last night after Emma left, he was still missing and his parents were worried sick.

He stared at the dark opening in the wall and then at his surroundings. He had no idea where he was or how to get out of there.

Above him were no manhole covers or other openings to the surface world. In the end, that was what made up his mind. Better to stay with Emma and Roger than to try and go off on his own.

"Hey, guys, wait up! I'm coming, too!" he yelled into the hole, and after tossing his baseball bat in and adjusting his hockey mask, he climbed in and began to crawl, his flashlight beam slicing through the darkness before him.

- 30 -

The tunnel became smaller after only a few feet, and was now no more than sixteen inches high. There was enough room to crawl but that was it.

As Emma continued onward, she tried to fight off the growing panic inside her. Thoughts of what would happen if Chad was right kept coming to the forefront of her mind.

What if it was a dead end? What would she do then?

She couldn't turn around, there was no room. She would have to back out inch by inch and that would take a long time. Her breathing was shallow as she crawled on, the flashlight cutting the darkness in half.

She wondered what she would do if her light gave out. She would be thrown into darkness, deep underground, with no way of knowing what was in front of her. If her light failed, she could crawl right into a group of rats and never know it until they were clawing out her eyes, tearing off her flesh, and feeding on her brains.

To die in the darkness would be a terrible way to go.

She began to shiver as the horrible thoughts began to rule her; she stopped crawling. She hadn't stopped for more than a few seconds before something pushed at her feet and she jumped in fear, actually striking her head on the tunnel ceiling.

It wasn't hard, but she saw pinpricks of light for a few seconds.

"Hey." It was Roger's voice coming from right behind her. "You okay up there? Why are you slowing down? Do you see something?"

She closed her eyes and gathered herself, pushing down the fearful thoughts, the weaker thoughts. Instead, she thought of revenge, of getting vengeance for her family and for Domenic.

She let the rage build up inside her, the stronger emotions quelling the other thoughts. When she was feeling better, she said, "I'm fine, I just needed a second to rest." She began crawling again.

- 31 -

Emma crawled for what seemed like forever but was in fact only another fifteen minutes or so. When she was beginning to feel like she had made a really huge mistake in diving in after the wounded rat, her flashlight beam suddenly widened and she found herself at the end of the small tunnel.

Her head was sticking out and she looked up, seeing a tunnel about six feet high and four feet wide before her. When she looked down, the floor was three feet off the ground.

Quickly, she slid out, falling out and whacking her knees on the rough cement that was the floor. She didn't care, she was too relieved to be in what appeared to be a massive opening after being in the cramped tube.

Roger stuck his head out a second later. He looked around for a moment and crawled out, tossing the baseball bat out first and handing the bucket of balloons to Emma. He slid out, landed on his hands and expertly used them to walk a foot. When his knees were clear, he pulled them close and his feet dropped out. Emma thought how easy he made it look and told herself she should have done that as well.

A half minute later, Chad's hockey-masked face appeared. He dropped his bat and slid out like an eel, landing and rolling to his feet. He pulled off the mask and wiped his brow with his arm. "Man, it's good to take this thing off."

"Then why'd you have it on in the first place?" Roger asked.

Chad shrugged. "I wasn't taking any chances. This thing save me once. If something came at me head on, I wanted to be ready for it."

"But me and Emma were in front of you," Roger said. "For something to get to you it had to go through us first."

"Yeah, I know," Chad said and walked away to examine their new surroundings.

Roger walked over to Emma and touched her arm. "How are you doing?"

"We lost the rat," was all she said.

"Hey, guys, I found something over here," Chad called.

- 32 -

Chad was standing ten feet into the tunnel, only his silhouette visible unless the flashlight beam was directed straight at him.

When the others joined him, he pointed down with his flashlight. The beam illuminated hundreds of human bones. They littered the floor from concrete wall to concrete wall.

All were small…the size of children.

As Emma stared in horror, she couldn't help but wonder what bones belonged to her baby sister.

With Chad leading the way, they began walking, following the carpet of human bones as if it was a trail. Soon they entered a large section of the sewer, and before them, eight rats stood blocking the way, their heads held high, eyes glowing against the flashlight beams.

"Oh shit," Chad whispered. He quickly made sure his hockey mask was on tight and held his aluminum bat in his hands. "Put your lights down so we'll be able to see or we're screwed."

They knew he was right. If their lights broke and they were plunged into darkness, it would be all over. They would never be able to fight without the use of their sight.

Each of them slowly placed their flashlights down on the ground and off to the side, the beam angling in different directions but allowing them to still see.

"There's no turning back now," Roger said. He put the bucket of gas balloons to the side and held his wooden bat aloft. "If we try to run they'll take us down from behind." He glanced at Emma. "We need you to fight with us, too. There's too many for only me and Chad to handle by ourselves."

"I'm ready," she said, her eyes cold, her jaw firm. After tucking the butcher knife into the belt on her pants, she reached into her duffle bag and pulled out the hedge clippers.

It was as if the rats heard her statement and took it as their cue to attack. In pairs of two they came at the three invaders in their home, hissing and screeching.

Chad was the first to engage the rodents, two rats coming for him with mouths open wide, teeth glinting in the gloom. He swung the bat like he was at home plate and was going for a homerun. The bat connected with the lead rat's head and cracked the skull in two.

Brains shot out of the gash to splatter onto the rat beside it. This one hissed in anger and prepared to leap onto Chad, but the bat was already coming around again on Chad's backswing. The blow wasn't as hard as the first one, but it was enough to daze the rodent.

As the rat shook its head and paused for a heartbeat, Chad raised the bat high and brought it down in a downward chop. The head was forced into the carpet of bones, a tiny femur impaling it under its chin. It spasmed and twitched as it dropped to the tunnel floor and died.

Breathing heavily, Chad turned to face his next attacker.

Meanwhile, Roger was battling three of his own, one rat leaping up and latching onto his chest.

He screamed as the claws dug deep into his skin but he didn't fall down. Balancing on the balls of his feet, he swung his wooden bat as hard as he could.

There was a dull thump when the tip of the weapon struck bone and a second later a rat fell limp with a broken neck. He kicked out with his right foot and managed to strike another one. He sent it spinning across the bone carpet to hit the wall hard.

With no others trying to get him, he then dealt with the one on his torso. The rat was trying to bite him and had already managed to nick his chin a few times. Only by moving about was he saved, the rat not able to get a good grip on his throat.

Using the bat, he spun it and held it in both ends, then jammed the center into the rat's mouth. Teeth scraped into the wood as he pushed harder and harder.

Spittle flew out of the sides of the rodent's mouth, hitting him in the face, but he ignored it.

Gritting his teeth, he dealt with the pain of the rat's claws as he slowly pushed the bat deeper and deeper into its maw. Then came a soft *crack* and the rat spasmed, its jaw becoming dislocated. Its

128

claws let go and it fell off him to land on its feet. Roger jumped on the rat's back so it looked as if he was riding it like a horse. After switching the position of his hands, he now began pulling back on the bat, the weapon still lodged deep in the rat's mouth.

His arms began to strain as he groaned with the exertion but he refused to let up. When he thought he couldn't keep it up, there was a wet *snap* and the rat's spine cracked in half. The pulsing thing between his legs immediately went still as blood seeped out of its mouth to roll over the bat and drip onto the gnawed bones at its feet.

Roger moved his head back and forth to see where Emma was in the dim illumination of the flashlights. He found her a second later.

She was at the mouth of the tunnel, and three rats had surrounded her and were about to attack. Though he jumped up and was ready to go to her aid, he already knew that whatever assistance he could give would come too late to help her. And Chad was also too far away.

Whatever happened next, Emma would have to see it through on her own.

- 33 -

Emma held the hedge clippers before her as the rats trapped her in the middle of a circle. Though she was scared, she remained calm, knowing if she panicked she would be dead.

She focused on the moment, not on the past, and that gave her clarity. She had done the same thing on the catwalk with Roger the previous day and had come up with a plan for escape.

Now, she held the hedge clippers wide open before her and waited for the rats to make a move.

She didn't have to wait long.

The shears in her hand were sharper than even Emma knew. Her aunt had always had a thing for sharp blades, saying that if they weren't sharp, then what were they good for? Every spring she would bring her hedge clippers, pruning blades and lawn-mower blade into a small shop in town which would hone them to razor sharpness.

So when the rat standing before her made the move to attack, and jumped into the air, going right for her throat, Emma raised the shears and pushed them forward. The rat's head slid past the closing blades and its neck became caught. But not for long.

Closing the shears as hard as she could, the razor sharp blades sliced through the rat's neck like it was soft butter, the head flying off to roll away as the body simply dropped at Emma's feet. Blood shot out of the neck hole to splash her legs, the warmth soaking in to override the feeling of coldness from the water that had already soaked her to the bone.

She didn't admire her handiwork, but turned to her right when she spotted movement out of the corner of her eye. Another rat was coming for her.

She was ready and when it lunged for her, she used the shears and sliced off its front legs, the rat hitting her in the chest to bounce off.

As it landed on its back at her feet, Emma leaned over and be-gan hacking away like the rat was a bush to be pruned. *Clack,* and another leg went flying off, then *clack, clack,* and the tail followed, along with the last leg.

The rat became nothing but a head and torso; it couldn't move. It squealed and hissed but it was dying of blood loss, and as it was, the rodent was harmless, unless she was careless enough to get too close to the snapping jaws.

She turned to face the last rat, which seemed to realize the odds had turned against it. It looked at its fallen brethren, at the three bloody children covered in rat blood, and decided that fleeing was better than dying.

It dashed past Emma as she tried to get it with the shears but the blades only managed to take off an inch of its tail.

This only made the rat run faster, spurred on by pain and imminent death. It raced past Roger and Chad, who each tried to whack it with their bats. It was too fast. It headed down the tunnel, dripping blood from its tail as it ran.

Roger joined Emma. "You okay? That was some work you did with that thing." He pointed to the bloody shears.

"I know, huh? I barely remember doing it," she said.

"Maybe it's time we left," Chad suggested as he joined them. "We've killed a lot of them, maybe they'll leave us and the other kids alone now." Though it was wishful thinking on his part, he still hoped Emma would agree.

She didn't. "No way. If anything, we proved they aren't indestructible. They can be killed. We're close now, I know it. These bones on the floor are proof. This get's finished, here and now." She picked up her duffel bag and one of the flashlights and began taking the same route the rat had used to escape. "Come on, let's go, we're wasting time."

Roger looked at Chad, who returned his gaze.

"You know, there's a chance she's gonna get us all killed," Chad said.

"Maybe, but I doubt it. Haven't you been paying attention? We're kicking ass here, man. Nothing can stop us." He picked up the two flashlights and tossed Chad one of them, and with a slight grin, turned and followed Emma.

Chad waited for only a second, then quickly ran after Roger and Emma. "I have a bad feeling about this," he mumbled under his breath, only the gnawed bones and rat carcasses there to hear him.

- 34 -

They were on the hunt now, Emma still in the lead. The carpet of human bones began to thin out, leaving the tunnel floor bare. Minutes later, they came upon a large room with four separate openings, five feet circular.

The second Emma entered this room, she saw it was basically a hub for the rats to go off in all directions, a nexus point for them to get access to the entire town.

In the center of the room, on a cement platform covered in debris such as newspaper and cardboard, as well as old clothes, was an image that caused Emma to gasp and the other boys to mutter silent curses.

The dais was surrounded on all sides by water, and on the platform was the largest rat Emma had ever seen. It was as big as a full grown horse, with dark black eyes and fur that was as white as a silk sheet. Its tail flicked fitfully as it stared at them. Surrounding the queen rat were more than three dozen smaller ones, most looking as if they were newborns.

More than half had no hair, their pink bodies constantly twitching as they tried to get at the nipples of milk each rat so desperately wanted, suckling and mewling constantly.

"Christ, it's some kind of mutant rat," Roger whispered from Emma's side.

At first Emma only had eyes for the queen rat, but after a moment, she moved her flashlight beam to the farther shadows, where the light illuminated the reflection of dozens of black eyes.

"I think we found the nest," Emma breathed as she stared at the rats around her. They didn't move, didn't so much as twitch as they stared at the three intruders that had dared to invade their innermost sanctum.

"That's fucking great," Chad whispered. "But what do we do now? Jesus, there's too many to fight. They'll overrun us in seconds."

Emma's mind was working overtime as she tried to think how best to deal with the present situation. She looked at the queen, at the rats surrounding her, and then at the debris the queen was using as bedding. It wasn't wet like most things in the sewer were, the bedding was nice and dry...too dry actually. One spark would be all it'd take to set the entire thing ablaze.

She began to take a mental inventory of all the items she and the boys had with them. Hedge clippers, baseball bats, the butcher knife, the cherry bombs Roger had told her about earlier and most of all, the bucket filled with gas balloons, that were even now beginning to break as the gas ate through the rubber.

And then she had it, the entire scenario snapped into her head as if someone had formulated it in order and placed it there.

Turning to Roger, she said, "Get out those cherry bombs and start lighting and throwing them at the rats. The noise should be enough to distract them for a few seconds."

"And what are you gonna do?" Roger asked.

She took the bucket of gas balloons from him.

"Get even," she said and turned to Chad, ordering him, "You help Roger. I just need a minute."

Chad said nothing, only staring at the rat queen in amazement.

"Chad, snap out of it," she hissed. "I need your help."

"Huh? Oh shit, sorry, it's just..."

"Yeah, I know. Help Roger." She turned to Roger. "You better throw them now, I don't think we have any more time left." She was now looking at the larger black rats surrounding the queen as they began to move closer to the three invaders.

Roger's hands dove into his pockets and he began taking out the cherry bombs in handfuls. He handed a pile to Chad and a cigarette lighter. A few fell out of the sides of his hands and rolled around at his feet.

On the dais, the queen rolled to her side and sat up. She was far too large to move and Emma had to wonder how she had gotten into this larger room. She surely hadn't fit through one of the tunnels.

But then she remembered the rats that had attacked her in her home and how they had squeezed through the smallest places. Where ever the queen had come from, the tunnels would have been easy for her to traverse.

The queen's eyes bore into Emma's and for just a fraction of a second, it was as if she could read the massive rodent's mind. It said, "You're dead for coming here!"

The queen then let out a screech that had every rat jump into action. Like a black wave, they came out of every hole, every crevice, all racing at the three children.

"Light them now!" Emma yelled and dropped to her knees to dig in her duffel bag.

"Oh shit, I knew this was a bad idea!" Chad screamed and began to light fuses, then chucked them underhanded at the coming swarm.

Roger was doing the same, and with each toss of his wrist, a cherry bomb flew through the air.

They landed on the backs of the lead rats and exploded a second later. The mini-grenades were more than enough to break the charge of black fur and the rats scattered in all directions, the ones in the back scrunching up as they ran into their halted brothers and sisters.

Again and again, the two boys threw the burning fireworks, and moments later the loud bangs of the explosives filled the cavern. A cherry bomb could blow a toilet in half, and with more than two dozen being lit and ignited almost at once, it sounded like a small war was occurring.

Not that a small war happening wasn't far from the truth.

Some of the cherry bombs blew up on heads and landed at feet, the force of the small blasts enough to split bodies open and shatter skulls when they landed directly on their targets.

Many of the rats were bleeding and confused, not understanding what was going on, a few lashing out at one another in their confusion, taking out chunks of flesh from their brethren's hides.

Emma found what she wanted in her duffel bag, and she pulled out the blowtorch. Using the BBQ lighter, she lit the torch, then placed it beside, her, the torchlight breaking the darkness.

All their flashlights were on the ground once more, the diffuse beams causing shadows to flicker across the walls, as if more giant rats, some the size of houses, were coming for them. Some rats had silver tags on their ears, but most did not, the new generations growing with each passing week.

Emma reached into the bucket of gas balloons and pulled a few out, cradling them like newborn babies in the crook of her arm. They dripped gas over her arm and she could smell the fumes, but she ignored it. The balloons felt like they would break at any second and she said a silent prayer that they would last for a few more seconds.

"Hurry up, Emma!" Chad screamed. "Do something if you're gonna do it!"

She did.

She got as close as possible to the queen, then began throwing the gas balloons at her. They arced through the air to hit her on the side, the neck, her haunches.

Emma went back for more and threw them as well, most coming short and only splashing on the debris the nest was made of. That was fine with her, too.

The baby rats were going wild as the gas burned their pink skin. The queen was also flailing, her high-pitched screams loud enough to make the three children want to get on their knees and cover their ears, the sound penetrating into their very psyche.

The black rats that were the queen's army redoubled their attack and charged en masse, more than half reaching the two boys.

Using the last of the cherry bombs, Roger and Chad dropped their lighters and picked up their baseball bats, then began swinging for all they were worth. They fought as if their lives depended on it, because it did.

Emma had used up the rest of the gas balloons, and she took the bucket and threw it at the queen. The bucket spun end over end and landed on her back, then bounced and fell off. The gas that had seeped out of the balloons splashed her, further adding to her saturation.

But Emma's plan was far from finished, and in fact, the hardest part was still to come. She had added the incendiary, but there was no way to light it properly, though she did come up with a reckless idea.

Then an afterthought came to her, a better way to light the gas than her first idea. She wished the boys had saved one cherry bomb, for they could have thrown it at the queen and its explosion hopefully would have done the job of setting the gas ablaze, but the firecrackers were all used up.

So much for planning, she thought. But she still had her crignal idea, the one she had planned on using, and with no other options, she put it into action.

Picking up the blowtorch, careful not to get it too close to her, knowing the fumes surrounding her, and the gas that had soaked into her clothes was dangerous, she held the torch at arm's reach.

With determination locked onto her face, she began to run straight at the queen.

- 35 -

Roger saw Emma dash past him. "Emma, get back here! What the fuck are you doing?" he called out.

She ignored him, and charged right into the encroaching rats.

As soon as she entered their fray, they began to attack her, biting at her legs, scratching her, trying to climb onto her back. One rat jumped onto the back of another so it was chest high with her.

She used the blowtorch and thrust it at the rat's face, the flame burning its eyes, melting the black orbs within and setting its fur ablaze. The rat screeched in agony and fell away to be lost in the tidal wave of bodies.

It was like walking through the sea against the current, each inch of ground fought hard for. Her only saving grace was the rats were so confused that most didn't realize she was within their midst.

Another jumped up and sank its teeth into her shoulder, then with its claws climbed higher and bit the back of her neck. She cried out as teeth sank a half inch deep but then twisted and used the torch to burn off her attacker. As it let go, she reached around and grabbed it with her free hand, her fingers wrapping around its neck. She squeezed as hard as she could and the rat's neck gave way, the cartilage no match for a girl filled with rage and vengeance. She dropped the carcass and fought onward.

Before Emma, the queen rose up on her hind legs, her head brushing the ceiling, and squealed loudly, the echo reverberating throughout the sewer. Emma didn't know how she knew this, but she was sure the mother rat was calling all its babies home to defend her, if there were any still out there.

It took less than a minute for Emma to reach the platform of the queen rat, but to her it felt like it had taken hours. She stood before the dais, almost as if she was supplicating herself. The babies mewled and squeaked, not understanding what to do, some still blind from birth, others in agony from the dousing of gasoline.

Emma looked up at the queen, and for a second halted, both hunter and prey locking eyes. The queen's eyes widened, and she hissed angrily at the small girl that was causing her so much pain.

The queen rat leaned forward and swiped a white paw at Emma, who jumped away at the last second, rolled a few feet away, and came up in a half crouch. She glanced around her to see there were no black rats nearby, none this close to the queen. She looked over her shoulder to see Chad and Roger all but buried under a wave of dark fur, their bats coming up and down again and again.

When she looked back, the queen was before her, having slid to the very edge of the platform. Her head was raring back, preparing to snap down and take off Emma's head like it was a lollipop, to then bite her in half and devour the young meat that had been so foolish as to try and defy her in her own sanctum.

But before the queen could attack, Emma threw the blowtorch, the canister spinning end over end in the air.

"That's for my family, you bitch!" Emma screamed, the yell so loud it burned her throat with its intensity.

The blowtorch arched high and almost hit the ceiling, and for an instant Emma thought she had thrown it too hard, that it would keep going and fall behind the platform, but then it reached its ascent and tumbled straight down to land at the queen's legs, the flame still burning bright.

The gas-soaked debris of the nest ignited on contact, and in seconds was consuming the giant white rat and its babies.

A giant *whoosh* consumed the oxygen in the chamber, the queen squealing in pain. As the call for help went out, every rat in the chamber stopped attacking Chad and Roger and turned and raced back to their queen.

One at a time they jumped to her aid, their mindless devotion their undoing.

As they joined her, they began to burn, the odor of burned meat and singed flesh filling the cavern as every rat was consumed; dozens upon dozens of bodies feeding the flames.

In the center of the funeral pyre, the queen's skin began to bubble and pop, and the white hair burned off as it was swallowed by the gas-fueled flames.

The smell was unbearable and Emma covered her face with her arm, knowing she would never get the smell out of her nose. That the odor would haunt her for the rest of her life, and even when she was an adult, there would be days that the odor would come to her on its own volition, bringing back the memory.

Soon, the entire chamber was burning. The smoke choked Emma as she backed away to join Chad and Roger, who were covered in yet more rat blood but looked no worse for wear.

Roger, not having the benefit of hockey gear, had a few more wounds on him than Chad, but he was intact.

He stood breathing heavily, the baseball bat hanging heavily from his hand like a bloody sword. He would be getting shots he knew, no doubt one for rabies. He wasn't looking forward to it, especially after the stories his father had told him.

"We need to get out of here!" Roger yelled when Emma joined him. Her pants were ripped to shreds from claw swipes and blood could be seen seeping through the holes, but none of her wounds were fatal, though a few may have needed stitches. The bite on the back of her neck had already clotted.

Smoke had filled the cavern to the point all three of them had to drop down on their knees or suffocate.

"Which way do we go?" Emma yelled while coughing, her sense of direction completely haywire.

Chad crawled over to her and Roger. He had a flashlight in his hand. "Follow me, I think it's this way." He turned and began to crawl away. Emma followed, then Roger, the three of them crawling like babies that had just become mobile.

Minutes later, Chad reached the tunnel entrance and all three got to their feet and began to run. The smoke still hung in the air but the further they got from the flames, the easier it was to breathe.

By the time they reached the carpet of bones and the dead rats they'd killed before, they were breathing without coughing. Roger had snot running down his nose and chin. He wiped it away with the back of his arm.

Chad led the way with the only remaining flashlight. Somewhere along the way he'd lost his bat but Roger still had his.

Emma had left her duffel bag as well, but she still had the butcher's knife jammed into her pants.

None of them said a word, only trudged onward, ignoring the water they splashed on one another as they clomped through the sewer, dragging their feet in exhaustion.

Each was lost in his or her thoughts, too traumatized by what they'd experienced to want to talk.

It took half an hour to find an opening they could use to escape the sewer, as most of the manhole covers couldn't be opened.

The covers had been unused for so long that they were practically glued to the ground, and only by having leverage from the top would they become cracked and opened.

As they stepped out of the sewer opening and into the bright light of early morning, they found themselves on a side street about a block from their school.

The street was empty which was fortunate, for each of them was covered in soot from head to toe, as well as generous helpings of dried blood.

They looked as if they had participated in a slasher film and had gone home without showering.

They stood looking at one another for more than a minute, before Emma reached over and gave Roger a hug, then Chad.

"I don't know how to thank you, guys. I don't know how we managed it, but we did it. We killed them all," she said, tears welling up in the corners of her eyes.

"Well, I think Domenic would be proud of what you did back there," Chad said.

She nodded. "You two know we can never tell a soul about what we've done, right?"

Roger chuckled. "As if there was any doubt. Hell, I doubt anyone would believe me even if I tried." He glanced down at himself. "I think I want to go home now and take a shower for a week."

They turned together and began walking down the street. A few streets over, they could see wisps of smoke rising into the air and the sound of a fire engine in the distance.

Emma walked between Chad and Roger, and she reached out her hand to each of them.

They took her hand and she squeezed Chad's, then Roger's, then raised them over her head like she was cheering. She did this for just a few seconds.

As she lowered them, still not letting go, they began their trek home, side by side.

Epilogue

When fire services finally made it into the sewer and found the site of the fire, there was nothing left but ash and animal bones and the scorched blowtorch, which looked as if it was only trash that been caught in the inferno.

When the small human bones were found, no one understood what it meant, but before anyone could question the discovery, mysterious men in black arrived and locked down the site, taking charge and sending any personnel not relevant away.

Dr. Saunders and Connors were there, as were many others that were part of the team.

The cover-up had begun…again.

For days the site was scrubbed clean, the human bones taken out in plastic boxes. Larger tents were erected over manhole cover openings so no one could see what was removed.

When the last person did one last walkthrough and finally exited the sewer, satisfied that the cover-up was complete and that their secrets were intact, the sewer system fell into silence.

But if someone had remained and stayed quiet, so that no one knew they were there, the person would have detected a noise other than the dripping of water.

A soft sound could be heard, and if it was followed through the sewer lines to its source, about a quarter mile away from the fire, a squeaking could be heard.

If there had been someone there to see it, the person would have looked up near the ceiling, to a broken pipe no more than six feet in diameter, to see the face of a white rat appear, one slightly larger than an ordinary one.

The female rat sniffed the air, and satisfied it was alone, retreated back into its sanctuary

The rat knew it needed to rest.

It was pregnant.

It was almost time.

ZOMBIE BUFFET: AN UNDEAD ANTHOLOGY
Edited by Anthony Giangregorio

If you're hungry for zombie stories, look no further than this anthology. There's enough rotting meat to satisfy even the most discerning connoisseur, and our all-you-can-eat buffet is sure to please.
Rotting intestines, severed heads and exploding spleens are just some of the courses waiting for you within this book of undead mastication.
So grab a knife and fork, slap on a napkin, 'cause you're gonna get dirty, and prepare yourself for the Zombie Buffet.
A zombie feast of epic proportions.

DEAD CHRISTMAS: A ZOMBIE ANTHOLOGY
Edited by Anthony Giangregorio

Share the most special time of the year with someone you love, or better yet, with an animated corpse!
The living dead love Christmas. Whether they're hanging their entrails like garland, using severed heads like stockings, or hanging body parts like ornaments, even zombies enjoy the most wonderful time of the year.
Santa Claus isn't immune to the walking dead, either.
Zombie elves, killer reindeer and undead hordes, all seek to share in the joy of the holiday . . . and tear Santa apart and feed on his flesh.
So when you grab last year's fruitcake to re-gift to Aunt Martha, just make sure to bring a shotgun, too. Because for all you know, your aunt has turned into an undead flesh-eater, and if the shotgun won't kill her, the fruitcake most assuredly will.

BIGFOOT TALES
Edited by Mark Christopher

The elusive Bigfoot has been a mystery for years.
Truth or hoax? No one knows for sure and perhaps never will.
So does this creature of the forest truly exist? Is there really a missing link that ties together man with his ape ancestors?
Or is it all simply a figment of the imagination.

ZOMBIES, MONSTERS, CREATURES OF THE NIGHT

OPEN CASKET PRESS

OPEN CASKET PRESS.COM

THE NEW NAME IN HORROR

THE PLACE TO GO FOR ZOMBIE AND APOCALYPTIC FICTION

LIVING DEAD PRESS

WHERE THE DEAD WALK
www.livingdeadpress.com

CLAN OF THE BIGFOOT

ANTHONY GIANGREGORIO

www.ingramcontent.com/pod-product-compliance
Lightning Source LLC
Chambersburg PA
CBHW071000120726
47910CB00004B/1315